IN PRAISE

OF LOVE AND CHILDREN

D0112315

BERYL GILROY

IN PRAISE
OF LOVE AND CHILDREN

PEEPAL TREE

First published in Great Britain in 1996
First reprinted 2002
Peepal Tree Press Ltd
17, King's Avenue
Leeds LS6 1QS
Yorkshire

ISBN 0 948833 89 0

IN LOVING MEMORY OF
P.E. GILROY
1919-1975

Acknowledgements

Many thanks to my daughter Darla-Jane for insisting that I publish this work that has been in process for many a year, to Christine King for her recognition of this work as literature, and not just as 'Black Literature', to Chantal Stanley for translating 'The Lotus', to Joan Anim-Adoo for 'reading trials' at Goldsmiths, to Jeremy Poynting for his integrity in dealing with our works that have been marginalised for years, and to my friends and critics Dr Mary Conde, Susheila Nasta, Dr Carole Boyce-Davis, Professor Adele S. Newson, Dr Linda Robeson, Dr Jagdish Gundara, Professor Ken Ramchand and my son Professor Paul Gilroy of Yale and Goldsmiths Universities. Special thanks to Dr. Daryl Dance and Dr Jacqueline Stephens for sustained encouragement through my times of self-doubt.

SECTION ONE

Those peaceful days of swaying trees and branches,
When dew-pearls shine on early leaf
And wanton maids seek assignations,
When birds devour insect feasts,
and glass-backed fish leap to morning sun,
I sing into a damsel-wind.
A butterfly's kiss, my fragile tune;
Soundless notes to reckless ears;
A sojourner's call —
A life's lament, that song I bring.
I give my offering of tears,
and move towards gold-beaded years.

CHAPTER 1

'Those peaceful days of swaying trees and branches...' Mrs Jocasta Penn, my teacher and mentor, had written those words which had come to her on the waves of a dream. She bade her students commit them to memory to challenge themselves with, and I had grown to rely on their music when either uncertainty or dread gripped me, as they did on the day of my arrival in London.

I stood on Paddington Station amongst its swarming life — unbelieving, yet conscious of a boundless joy. My breath came softly, slowly, to form the words, 'At last! I'm here! I've come! We're together, London and I!' But where was Arnie, my brother, who had left us six years earlier to fill a menial niche here? He had promised to meet me. Now where was he? On Nation Time perhaps – that indefinite time, when we renounced the clock and came and went as we liked! The sun was our clock at home but there was no sun in this English August. I craned my neck to see through any break in the frenetic panorama, my doubts whipped up like wind-blown water.

Had Arnie come and gone unrecognised? Had he left me lone and lost in London town? Then I saw him coming towards me, measuring the ground with even, loping strides, a jaunty cap on his head. The same sharp, pointed chin, the same beetle-brown eyes too large for that size of face, the hands pushed into the pockets like a spade into the earth. The smooth, grey coat gave him a parcel-wrapped look; I was sure it did not belong to him. He smiled swiftly. Now dark, now glowing like fish scales at night.

'Hello, Sis! Sorry I'm late. Shift work. By the time I get up, wash and shave, the hour past and gone.'

I could not contain myself, so flooded with delight I was! He looked more handsome than ever. I hugged him, kissed him, taking in the ripe-fruit smell of his sweat and breath, and then, remembering Ma and the others, I sobbed a little. But Arnie, inured from childhood to the sighs and sobs of women, let the sounds fall and die in the dust.

'You look rich!' I cried. 'Smooth grey coat! Cap and all!' He smiled and led me off to the taxis.

'This is all you have, Sis? This suitcase and these few etceteras?' he asked, as if switching on a light inside him.

'Yes, Arnie. That will do for now.'

We queued for a taxi. Suddenly, stories, news, messages that had to be told sprouted by the dozen in my mind and, in spite of myself, I began to pour them out right there, in the queue, with the din of buses, cars and voices all around me. Heads turned. Someone snarled, 'Shut up!' I obeyed, leaving unsaid half-formed words hovering between us like hummingbirds over hibiscus flowers. I was glad to climb into the shelter of a black taxi.

Buses as big as houses on wheels passed close by, and I wondered where all those people, with never a smile or wave to anyone, were going.

The taxi driver said a few words to Arnie, who gave him further directions.

'Not far now, Sis,' Arnie said. 'Soon there.'

I was almost a guest in Arnie's home!

We stopped outside a brick house with a single roof but with two sets of windows and doors. Two houses under one roof!

'This,' Arnie explained, 'is what people here call a "semi-detached" because one wall fasten to the other house.'

'I see, Arnie, I see. You mean they share a common wall?'

'Hm,' he replied as he hunked the suitcase into the open door. It tipped on its side with a mild clatter in the hallway.

'Upstairs, Sis. We live upstairs.'

I climbed the steps. Not just a few like I was used to, but plenty — twenty or more.

'Be careful of the holes in the carpet, Sis. Don't let them catch your heels! Wear and tear, you know. Push open the door in front of you.'

I obeyed. The room that came to view was neat, with a bed, a dressing-table, a wardrobe and another chair and table. All very still and stubborn-looking.

'You live in a half-a-house, Arnie?'

'No, in half a half-house. This is my flat. Two bedrooms. I'm very lucky. People have nowhere to live since the war bomb out everything.'

I sat down on the bed. It felt good but wood hard.

'I will make tea,' said Arnie. 'Here, everyone drinks tea. Like coconut water back home.' As he laughed, some secret pleasure came out in a hiss through the gap, as wide as ever, between his two front teeth.

'No thanks! No tea for me. Water will do. Forget the coconut.' We both giggled like children.

'Smell this,' Arnie said, turning on a tap on the cooker. 'It's gas. It can kill. You must never forget to light it.'

'And if you run out of matches?'

'Then don't turn it on. You hungry?'

'No. I'm full of thoughts. Too full to eat.'

'Well, if you change your mind, some stew is in that pot there.'

'So you can cook!'

'You have to, Sis, or you live on fish and chips and that's not always good. Besides, you get fed up with the smell of fish.'

I walked round the flat, looking into the state of it. It not only contained every convenience, but everything was close. At home, in our village, the latrine was outside. Here it was actually in the bathroom.

'You like my place, Sis?'

'Yes, Arnie. Of course.'

'It's my place,' he said proudly. 'When I come in and shut the door, nothing can trouble me. Took me a long time to find it.'

He chuckled softly. 'I have to go to work now. Time come.'

'Where do you work?' I asked.

'At a bakery. I'll be back at around ten tonight. I have to mix an ocean of dough. I can mix and make the bread, but I can't sell it to white people in the shop. Here's the key.'

So there I was, left all on my own in Arnie's flat at two o'clock in the afternoon.

As I had a key, I decided to go out and explore. I walked down the street until I came to a market. It had a challenging variety of goods. To buy was to choose, and I had never learned to choose. With its countless stalls and the special uniforms worn by the fishmongers, bakers and even the coal-vendor selling coal by the bucket to the poor, it was a truly fascinating place. The smells, the banter, men eagerly hefting bags of vegetables — all gave me a sense of pleasure hard to describe. But the greyness of the clouds, the solid look of the buildings and the closeness of the shops made me long for open space and sunshine.

The face of the main street was scrubbed by the wheels of buses and occasionally by those of cars. The dust rose slowly — lazily — unlike our scurrying, overpowering, easily-roused country dust. Compared with our shops at home, the market-stalls contained an astonishing variety of things. I had heard of wartime rationing, but evidently that was long over. I felt happy that I had come to a place where there was so much of everything — even if I had to work hard and wait for my share of it.

I drew my resolve about me as if it was one of those beautiful coats in a clothes' shop window. I was going to prove myself by my work, as generations of black women had done. My worth would be reflected by useful deeds for this great country. I could feel it in my bones. Excellence had been talked into me by Mrs Penn. Once more I could hear her singing in her soft, tuneful voice, 'I vow to thee my country, all earthly things above'. And to my way of thinking, 'all things here below' as well. I was far from home and free of those invisible cords that had bound me. I felt freedom for the first time in my life, a freedom made possible by Mrs Penn's final bequest to me. In death, as in life, she was my liberator.

Our family had consisted of Ma and Pa, the twins, Arnie, Jacko, Mattie, and me (Melda). The twins, Flora and Florizel, were as alike as two pretty peas in a pod. They were strange, able to communicate without words, each sharing only with the other.

Pa was a big man who had once shown fire, but with burden after burden had turned to dull coals which sparked only after a great deal of prodding. His hands, large enough to grab and hold four melons, fidgeted like automata accompanying his inner thoughts. His smile came slowly, as if excavated from granite. Tall and straight in youth, he had let his oncoming age settle on to his back, his willing shoulders and his cautious eyes, as if putting on display what he saw as reality, the insecurity he had known throughout his life.

Ma was a half-pint to Pa's pint. Everything had been matched in the making of her body, but in her mind she was always spiralling about or boring down as if trying to find and put the tangled ends of herself together.

Ma left the twins to their own devices, but Pa told them what would do and what would not. Arnie and I were very close in age, just a few months separated us; only later in life was I to understand how this could be. Jacko was independent and solitary, roaming the fields, and either fishing or playing cricket when not at school. Mattie, the youngest, was the centre of the concern and care of all of us. She had a weak chest. People called it asthma, and Ma gave her herbs to drink. I fetched them from our neighbour, Mama Tat, who was old and knew everything.

We lived in a large house made of crabwood boards with a thick hat of thatch for the roof. Ma had inherited the house from her parents. It was low and big with three steps to the front door and jalousies to let in the air. We had no glass windows.

Inside, our house consisted of a large family room, with a bedroom for Ma and Pa behind it. A little passage led to Arnie's and Jacko's room, containing two home-made bunks, and then on to a large room where all the older girls slept on a huge bed, beside which was a cot for Mattie. Pa put nails all around the walls for us to hang our few possessions, and in this way we knew where to find our school clothes. The kitchen stood loose, a few steps from the house. It was difficult to move between house and kitchen when it rained.

We sat in the family room to eat. Ma insisted that we sat together and ate what we had grown in the garden and she had cooked, with us girls to help her. Ma tried never to spend money. She kept it as close to her as her clothes.

She treated me differently. The twins were given time to idle. So were Arnie, Jacko and, of course, Mattie; but I always had work to do — like the donkey that turns the millstone from dayclean to dusk. Ma was a tightly compressed woman, who had once been very lovely. She spoke little and then in a brittle voice. It was as if she had been stood on end and the warmth, affection and happiness had drained out of her. Sometimes her thoughts came out as little squeaks, groans or incomprehensible words. If she spoke to anyone it was to the neighbours, and particularly to Mama Tat, who looked older than age.

A certain amount of resistance, disobedience and rudeness was expected of boys, and complaining about 'baiys' allowed Ma some degree of affiliation with women who also had recalcitrant 'baiys'. When Mama Tat said, 'Dem baiys, deh so own-way, own-way — Gawd pretect me liver from dem', Ma knew what she was talking about. All the yard wives agreed that bad boys affected the mother's liver, making it sour and sickish with worry!

On Saturday nights, Pa went for a talk, a pipe and a game of dominoes with the men in the church hall. Arnie accompanied him but quickly returned with some rum for Ma. She sat alone to drink, away from the lamp in the semi-darkness of the family room, as if gloom enhanced the power of rum. After a while, instead of barking orders in her normal way, she would gently thaw out, and enquire whether our clothes for Sunday church were ready, and whether we had visited the ancestral graves recently.

Ma had only a few distant relations besides Auntie Bet, her last remaining sister. When Auntie Bet visited, Ma was renewed in heart and spirit. She set about the washing, digging, weeding and cooking, without complaint. She was kinder even to me, giving me slices of cake instead of crumbs and slaps instead of blows.

Strange as it may seem, when Ma yelled at me or gave me an unexpected cut with a stick, I thought she did it for my own good, as children were so often told, when adults chose to beat or pummel them, whether from anger or crass self-indulgence. What was harder to cope with was the way Ma used her eyes as weapons of near destruction upon me, looking so searchingly at me that I thought she was trying to locate the most vulnerable parts of my body to obliterate them. She seemed, with those mad, piercing brown eyes of hers, to be seeing right into me, and willing to death whatever was good and growing in me. She did not pretend to love me.

I remember those eyes of hers, as if they were being pushed out of her head to move like searchlights over everything. I understood later that she was really looking back into herself, that she could not see us at all, for her eyes shone with tears that would sooner or later be pearling down her face. Sobs, hard and deep, would bounce out of her very centre, as she struggled to dismantle her fury and her pain. These were the times when she would whip someone until, after a while, her exhaustion and crumpled emotions would pull her to the floor and abandon her there.

When Pa knew that someone had been whipped, he showed his resentment by talking of 'going away', while Ma continued to teeter on the edge between sanity and lunacy — confusing past and present, or smiling or cowering in turn. We feared Pa's talk about 'going away', rather than 'going away to work', even more than Ma's fury. We were so afraid we couldn't speak about it. Even the twins swapped their schemings for minutes of silence.

Sometimes, Ma was as normal as she ever could be, but listless and careless, as if an important part of her mind and her life was starved of essential food. I thought then that if left to herself she would escape and wander the seven seas. When she was happy, some magical place inside her came alive, and she abandoned all constraints except her concern with money. On these days she sang quietly to herself, she crooned and smiled, and allowed a tenderness to enter her fingers as she stroked the cat.

At about eight o'clock on the night of my arrival in London, I went to bed but could not sleep. I was constantly pinched by the sounds of unfamiliar voices from downstairs. The sounds changed at intervals — laughter in various sharps and flats, music now loud and then soft. Anger, and then the laughter of reconciliation. Two adults had reduced life and living to idiosyncratic play.

At around eleven, Arnie arrived, carrying a new loaf.

'You still up, Sis?' he asked cheerfully.

'Yes, hard to sleep. With those two downstairs.'

'They're common-class English people. They don't care how they carry on. Fight! Fight! Cuss! Cuss! Jaw! Jaw! OK when you know what to expect. They have bad wars sometimes!'

I chuckled softly as I remembered our family wars. The twins against the rest of us, beating us down with grown-up cuss-words, while a cluster of curious women dropped work to listen, pretending horror at the fluency of the twins but really enjoying themselves.

Arnie disappeared into his room, and I overheard him slurping his hot cocoa from a saucer, as if a cup was not enough. I turned off the light, but little mutters and murmurs, squeaks and cries came from the recesses of the house, as if it protested as being occupied by people who did not really belong there. Us upstairs and them downstairs.

I still could not sleep and, wrapping myself in a warm blanket, I curled up in the armchair. I must have dropped off, for there I was when Arnie stirred and visited the bathroom. I climbed back into bed and curled up again. I am a well-fleshed woman and would never feel even a cupful of peas under my mattress, but that night it was like lying down on heaps of dead bones. I jumped up again, frightened that a skeleton was hiding there. Mama Tat, who told us jumbie stories, often talked of 'skellingtons' and their antics in the graveyard. I looked under the mattress. No skeletons. No real mattress either — Arnie just hadn't used as much bedding as I was used to at home. Now that I understood the hardness and pressure on my skin, I promptly fell asleep. 'Hard bed, hard life,' Auntie Bet once said.

Arnie was first up and dressed, sipping tea and breaking bite-sized pieces from the loaf of bread.

'It's good to break bread with you after all these years,' I said, as I stuffed the sweet taste into my mouth. Arnie watched me, and noticing my enjoyment said, 'My friends cut bread, you know, as if they never read the Bible. They take a saw-teeth knife to the bread. God, it jus' like cutting you mudda, I mean mother.' Actually he said 'murther' in his attempt to talk what was considered 'good English'.

'Yes, Arnie. Bread is life. You can't cut life.'

I didn't like the taste of the tea. I preferred coffee, but I didn't say anything. We were never allowed to complain or criticise others or what was offered to us.

Arnie put butter, peanut butter and jam on his bread like a rich man. Ma would have died at the sight of it. We had one at a time. It took three weeks to taste all three.

After he'd gone to work, I busied myself, putting the food away, dusting down the table before flies or ants could take over and prevent me from sorting out my papers, but, several hours later, not a fly or ant was in sight. Funny sort of place, I thought. Ants and flies are the salt of the earth.

I switched on the radio. The English words were nice to hear. Apart from the radio, I was alone, solitary in that box-room — like an island with me a castaway on it, and never a fly for company.

Suddenly, the downstairs door opened, and up the stairs came a tall, blonde woman with eyes as blue and hard as fossils of aquamarine. Our eyes made four and her thin, funny-coloured, string-bow lips shifted this way and that into a smile, which drew my eyes away from her limp, yellow hair.

'Hello. I am Trudi. Arnie is my friend. He told me so many wonderful things about you and his family. You had a good journey, *ja?* Ah, there is no mattress on your bed. We will get one today. It will be softer than sleeping on the floor.'

'Arnie was here all the morning, and he never mentioned you,' I replied stiffly. 'And Arnie always mention friends. What do you want, Mistress Lady?'

'I tell you, I am Trudi. I come to talk with you and make you comfortable and welcome.'

'I am fine, thank the Lord. He is the one I depend on.'

But she was determined.

18

'Here is a map. It help you go from place to place on the underground. Do you know the market?'

'You are not going to work, Mistress? Don't go late on account of me.'

'No. Till four o'clock. I have time to show you the market, then four clock I go to work with my quick feet.'

'Not today, if you don't mind. Another day, I will go to the market.' I gave her sixpennyworth of smile to make my point. Later I watched her go, her legs cutting space like scissors.

Sweat began to shine on my skin. What did Arnie want with a person like that? A mistress, who pay poor people twelve dollars a month to scrub and cook, throw old clothes at them, keep mothers away from their baby-children! I began to boil with passion. The nearest I had ever been to those people was the distance of the pulpit in church. Afterwards I would say a quick how-d'ye-do and give a quicker walk past. The more of 'them' around, the more I sweat.

Ma would have rushed straight to Mama Tat to complain about Arnie. Ma didn't even like Tim Walker, a half-black boy who used to come and roll on the grass with Flora and Florizel. They were about thirteen going on fourteen at the time — tall and well rounded with all their women's markings clear. Here the hips, here the waist — up yonder a pair of nicely shaped tangerine-sized breasts. Well, this boy used to come dressed in short pants, brilliantine hair, white shirt and whistling a tune! While the twins stood snickering and behaving stupid, he would give them thrown-out magazines to read. Every time Mr Walker took tourists to the reef in his boat, they gave Tim old magazines with love stories and brazen men and women in them. Tim and his partners in evil, Winston, Barrymore and Garfield, would get to peep at the pages and giggle and shout, 'See that swaga-boy with the hairy chest. That's me!'

'That one is me! That sweet-man!'

'No, me!'

After a while they would start hitting each other, pushing

and flicking Job's tears which grew wild nearby. If I showed up they would shout 'Melderella' at me, and tease me so much I could only hide and watch as Tim aimed his pebbles at the twins' breasts; and then the girls would grab Tim or one of the other boys and roll around on the grass and laugh hysterically. The twins loved whatever was going on, although I didn't realise it. I used to run and call Ma, and she would come with a stick and chase them home, saying they were too big to play such games. But raw brazenness swamped the twins like high-tide water, and showed in their motions and their actions in playing with this half-black, half-white boy.

Now here was Arnie with a woman who was not like his mother, his sisters or his headmistress. Even her eyebrows were blonde. Just to look at her made my skin grow gooseflesh and crawlish. What a sin! What a sight!

When Arnie came home he looked tired, but tired or not I called him to question.

'The mistress-woman came here, Arnie, and told me bold as brass she wanted to drag me to the market. If I want to go there, I would search till I find it, if I didn't know it already.'

'She's no mistress. She's a good, kind girl. She come from a place called Germany and she is displaced. Her family lived in East Germany and the communist take it over. She has an aunt in Switzerland and she goes home to them. She's a good person.'

'A good person? The ones that start the war? Hitler grand-daughter that only know how to say "heil this" or "heil that"? How you mean displace?'

'I never asked her; like I never notice all the things you notice. She is a nice girl and don't know anything 'bout black-hating and white-hating.'

'We lost our language. Not our eyesight. *They* all know colours, especially black and white.'

'Hm! Sis, you...'

'Is she your friend, your young lady or your playmate?' I

barked, not giving him time to finish.

'All three,' he said. 'You can learn from Trudi. She show me life in a different way. She teach me how to play. I never learned how to play. Never had time!'

'Well, good luck to you. Ma would fall down dead to hear such foolish words as that. And Pa? Well, he would kill you. We are black. Black and white make grey and you had all the time in the world to play.'

He sat down again and ate the rest of the leftover stew ravenously, as if trying to cover the doubts inside him. He stared at me but didn't speak. I could see his mind working. I could not, however, guess what conclusions he reached. He was a man now and very, very mannish, answering me back and arguing.

I said, 'I am going to find a post office. I have to let them know the kind of dance you're dancing. You hearing jumbie-voices. Doing jumbie-things!'

'It's just up the road, Sis. The post office. Stand in the queue.' He was ignoring me — pretending not to hear!

I walked gingerly down the stairs and, as I opened the door, who should be approaching but Mistress Trudi, a crocodile smile on her lemonish face.

'Hello, Melda, hello,' she began. 'You are going for a walk, *ja?* Wait till I give this to Arnie and I will come too.' She waved a small packet at me and then accompanied me to the post office. From time to time she nudged me, and prattled away in her language and then, realising her mistake, she would say, 'Of course, you do not know the German. I am so sorry. You have one language alone, English.'

I looked at her. 'Never smile with a crocodile,' Mrs Penn said, whenever she had to deal with bumptious people.

I had never thought of English in that way before. I began to smile.

'You are right. So many languages in the world and I only have English. I believe in English,' I said, still compressing

21

my lips but managing a laugh — well, a bit of a laugh.

Trudi laughed too. It was the first time we laughed together. But I did not and never could trust her. It was because of white people laying off men at the factory that poor Pa had to leave us to look for work in America.

I remember those dreadful times so well. Only Mattie had a present that Christmas. Pa could not even buy a cake of 'sweetsoap' for any of us girls, or a ball for Arnie and Jacko. Pa had come home covered with mud, carrying a small store bag, and we wondered what he had been doing. A few weeks later, voice rusty with worry, he called each of us by name and stood us in line. He gave us a small, ripe guava each, and said, 'Eat it when I'm gone. I am going to America to find work. I hear I could find good work there. I have plenty of friends there. Pray for your Pa. Eat your guava with love. Count the seeds. We'll be rich one day. Money is like guava seeds. We will have plenty.'

We started to cry. All at once. All together. Ma looked on helplessly.

'You have Ma.' He looked at her affectionately. 'And Ma have you.' He seemed emasculated, as if by the loss of whatever had made him a man.

'And God,' she added. 'He knows your future, Henry.'

'I will just go. I am not saying goodbye to no one in case I have to come back.'

We watched Pa go and when he was out of sight we tried to eat the guavas he'd given us. None of us could. Not even the twins who saw Pa as oppressive.

After Pa had gone, Ma relied a great deal on the women in the yards. They came and sat on our doorstep and talked of the men who had come and gone in their lives. Miss Daisie always started. She was self-pitying and pessimistic in her ways. 'Sancho left me. Years after saying he going out, I go to Port Mourant, I meet him there selling beef in the market. The man so fat I hardly know him after five years.'

'Oh, they know what is good for them! Charlie run off

with Doreen. Say to me, "You, gal, you too wanty, wanty".'

'He still come home, to die on my bed,' said Lucretia, giggling like a child.

The stories made me afraid of men, so I left them and went to the kitchen to make them coffee, or to fetch cakes from their houses or lock mongooses out of their chicken coops. But I could still hear their laughter or their sobs.

Pa wrote at last. He had got work and sent money for new clothes and canvas shoes for us.

Arnie and I grew closer together and talked of the future. I helped him understand things and grow in confidence. Like me, he read. We talked about books and laughed over characters in the stories we read. Then fate took a hand in our lives. Mrs Penn, the headmistress, sent a letter asking Ma for a visit. Ma was about her age, but she had married Pa at seventeen, and Mrs Penn had studied on and on, until she was appointed a headteacher. She married late in life — so late that she could not have children of her own, and instead became the mother of her school. Everybody loved her, praised her and listened to her wise, uplifting words. I believed her when she said, 'Dedication and ambition are twins,' and I began to foster both in myself.

The letter threw Ma in a spin.

'I know Mrs Penn from Redman Road where they lived in a range house,' Ma fumed, shaking her fist at her shadow. 'Mrs Penn's mother used to take in washing. What she want from me? Underneath my skin and bones, my washed-out clothes and my children, I am still Jacqueline Blackman married to Henry Hayley.'

It was the first time Ma had ever repeated her maiden name with the tiniest crumb of pride. Everybody knew her as Ma Hayley with the 'handsome red-skin boys and the nice-face black-skin girls', who baked party cakes for the village people and sometimes had sweets for sale. When we were all together, we were approved of as a beautiful crop of children.

Ma insisted that we cleaned the house from north to south and east to west. Even the rooms Mrs Penn would not see were cleaned as if for Christmas. When the house was ready, Ma sent Mattie to tell Mrs Penn 'to come anytime'.

On the day of Mrs Penn's visit, Ma was on edge and kept me home to tidy up the yard and sweep up the goat and pig doings, before Mrs Penn could give her a lecture on 'Yard Hygiene' or on 'Houseflies and Disease'. Mrs Penn came to our home after school in company with my brothers and sisters. The twins, Arnie, Jacko and Mattie, all in school clothes, behaved sedately. Jacko soon enough disappeared — he had a world in his head that could not be denied anything.

Mrs Penn entered our family room while Ma, extending a rigid hand, told her how glad she was to 'exchange words' with her after all the years. Mrs Penn hugged Ma and kissed her face. Ma reacted as if she was being smeared with dirt.

'You're blest, Jacqueline. You have left your mark in the world. These children are a credit to you.'

'What you come for? I was on tenderhooks for days. The children behaving with respect?'

'Oh yes! Oh yes! What I want to tell you is that I would like Melda to study with me three extra afternoons. I want her to pass her exam high. I want her for pupil teacher.'

Ma's face dropped like socks round her ankles. 'You come to see me 'bout Melda?' Her voice was sharper than a roll of barbed wire.

'Yes, Jacqueline. Melda has good brains and memory for facts and figures.'

Ma nodded and sat down by the door in a red-ripe state of anguish, her body in folds like a concertina.

'Melda! Melda!' she said, almost in a whisper.

I stepped forward and Ma suddenly turned on me.

'You little witch! Why you take away my daughters' clever-ness?'

'Ma! Ma!' Arnie shouted across her fury. 'Melda didn't dress. Melda wearing dirty clothes.'

'I don't care about that little... She is not mine! Take the twins! Not her! She's not mine!' Ma shrieked.

'I know she's not yours! Everybody does. You work her like a donkey from dawn to dusk. You're cruel to her. We all know,' Mrs Penn replied hoarsely.

Ma was not listening, only weeping, only pleading.

'Take the twins! They'll do what you want. They will! They are clever! They will learn. They are innocent angels. Innocent.'

'The twins will take a different road. They will do different things. They will cover you with worldly glory. Yes, they're innocent! Innocent as a god-horse, always praying over the dead creature it will eat.'

The twins winced and lowered their eyes. But Ma wept inconsolably.

I suddenly became aware of the smell of rubbish and dung. It was on my clothes, but Mrs Penn hugged me.

'Sorry, Melda, sorry if I acted wrong.'

After she left us, she crossed the yards, chatting with some, and talking deep with other women. Ma began to talk to herself.

'Mrs Penn's mother was a "come-to-see" just like her daughter. Everybody knew then. Just like salt-pork they were — always flavouring other people's food.'

Then Ma cried again as if she was in terrible pain.

The others had rushed away, leaving only guilty me and poor Ma, hunched up on the settee, clutching her shattered dreams.

What could we do except watch and wait? We wanted to be comforted, both of us. Our souls needed to hear the same music of solace and hope.

'Melda,' Ma said. 'Come.' Her voice was soft. I approached her hopefully, and she turned slowly, looked at me with those venomous eyes and struck me a thundering blow in my face. It caught my nose. At the sight and feel of the blood, I screamed, and Mrs Penn, hearing my screams, rushed back to our house. I staggered outside to the rainwater barrel, where I fell, moaning and desperate.

'You suffering child,' she said. 'A really bad fall! But it is not the end.' She led me back inside through the open door, comforting me with her touch. I could see Arnie kicking the water barrel, trying to maim it out of rage.

'Jacqueline,' Mrs Penn said, a sharp, serious edge to her voice, 'I know how sick-stupid you can be, but the twins have not got what it takes to study — so keep your hands off this child. Your twins are in the world — capering and clowning. Know that and be spared the pain of hopeless ambition.'

From that day, Mrs Penn became the fixed point of my existence and I measured out my life by her standards.

Ma began to call for Pa, or for her own pa — I didn't know which. And Mrs Penn, cradling her in her arms, rocked her backwards and forwards, saying calming words.

'Your pa died in the canes, Jacqueline. Died in the fire. Henry is your husband. Not your pa. The overseer dropped his cigarette and the blaze spread all over the dry grass.'

I sighed and opened a book but I could not read from the throbbing in my head. Poor me! Poor Ma!

Arnie entered the room and sat beside me. 'Don't cry, Melda. Don't cry.'

Now here was Arnie going to bed with the enemy who made his father leave home and turned Ma crazy. When Trudi showed up, I was abrupt with her. She made me so uneasy! She treated Arnie as if he was a white man painted black. She knew about white men — not about Arnie, who was raised poor with his parents struggling to get just enough food for all of us. She treated him like a man-dolly, dressing him up to look nice for her, just like the women in the yard and their grown-up sons, men who were adept at destroying anything — relationships, pride or their own ability to survive.

When Arnie's shift changed, she was in her element, wrapped round him every hour of the day. Then one day she went too far with me.

'Melda, why do you not get your own man, so you will not look so much at Arnie? What he does, what he think — eh?'

'I do not want a man. I am not interested in Arnie when he is under your hand. Men should rule. Not women!'

'Oh! Poor you! Missing the fun. Every woman wants a man if he cannot rule. OK, OK. Arnie does not want this ruling.'

'How do you know?' I barked.

'I can show you. There are always men in the pub. You can be special for them, if you do not be so sulky. You know yourself or you know Arnie? Which is this?'

'Oh for goodness' sake, Trudi. Do your embroidery.'

'This is needlepoint.'

'Well, do it and then go. I am going to the divisional office today to see if they give me a school. They are not telling me.'

'Good. Your mind will grow. Your mind is very narrow and you are always praying. Bleeding your knees. It is not only your knees. It is your heart.'

Arnie had told her how the women of the yards knelt on a grater to repent and cleanse away guilt through suffering.

'You mind your own business!' I shouted.

'It is my business. You are my sister-in-law-to-be! I want to help you to be better than what you are! The world is full of things to learn!'

I gave up and went out. Trudi, as frail and washed-out as she looked, had every move planned. It was a great relief to me when she finally went to work as a waitress at Lyon's Corner House and could visit only between her shifts.

CHAPTER 2

It turned colder. The leaves had brought a hurrying, scurry-ing, wind-blown beauty to the earth, creating a world of the unseen, the hidden, the mysterious. Where had summer gone, its roses and its colours? When Arnie came in, he sat down on my bed while I ironed or cooked for us and we talked of the weather and the trials of being so far from home.

'We are scattered all over the world, Sis. You and me over here. The others all over the place like the leaves outside. It is always autumn for some black people. Always. Scatter and scatteration!'

I said, 'The twins are money-minded, like Jacko aiming for all those dreams he keeps in his head. And Mattie — God knows! Life blowing us all here and there!'

'And Pa and Ma getting old in New York. I sometimes wonder what made Ma the way she was — so cruel, so violent, like slave days, Sis.'

'Slave-days is still with us, between man and wife, brother and sister, family and friend. When we fight with one another, we still in the slave-yards,' I replied.

'Some things about the yards I can't forget. When I talk to Trudi, she can't imagine them.'

'You talk to Trudi about us — about family?' I asked, dismayed.

'We compare. I told her about the goats.'

'Oh my God! You didn't tell her *that!* Ma was "going through"! She wasn't responsible. You shouldn't tell strangers about us. Especially about the goats!'

'Trudi is not a stranger.'

'She is your cousin? Your family?'

'No. She could be my wife.'

'Your wife! She could never be your wife! What you have that she wants? Think on it! You remember Uncle Dan who brought a white woman home? When he drowned, what she said? "Thank God Satan is dead. Now I can be myself".'

'That was not true. It came out of Mama Tat,' Arnie protested. 'She never called him Satan. She called him Judas Iscariot.'

'Well, don't tell your nearly-wife about your precious family who care about you, whatever husband call wife or vice versa. Our business is not a fairy story for her pink ears.'

'I am not bound to anybody,' Arnie replied crossly.

'You bound to your mother and father, and what is bound on earth shall be bound in heaven!'

'Oh, Sis, you just like Ma — full of Bible talk.'

If I'd had a place to go, I would have moved out there and then, but I had to put up with Arnie and his nonsense. I hated Trudi. We were at war only she didn't know it.

'This place so cold!' I shouted to no one in particular. 'Plug in the heater. God! This place so cold!'

The goat story was a particularly shameful one, and Arnie had no right whatsoever to talk against his mother to a stranger woman who looked like a plucked chicken in her colour. After all, who is a wife or a husband? A stranger you get children with. Ask Mama Tat!

Automatically I leaned over and scratched my shins. They were burning from ant bites all over again, so deeply angry was I about Arnie's betrayal. He had not been at home when it happened. He had heard it from me.

Ma had instructed the twins to milk her goats, two of them. But that very day, Barrymore, one of their admirers, had stolen some bright red nail polish from his uncle's drugstore and given it to them. Rather than spoil their nails, they let the goats escape, only to be milked by some villain from the yards. The goats had to be milked or they suffered painful udders, but Ma could not be reasoned with. She could not find the twins to punish, so she dragged me into the yard, smeared me with molasses, and stood me in an ants' nest, full to the brim with cutters that used to frighten us with their savagery.

The ants fell upon me, biting me with unrelenting ferocity. I screamed and ran to Mama Tat. What she did to me I cannot now recall, but though the itching went, I could not walk properly for days. After I was absent from school for several days, Mrs Penn sent a letter to Ma. Ma said I had walked on purpose into an ants' nest and, since no one doubted her, the matter died down.

After that, it was clear that Ma had become possessed by some larger and more incomprehensible evil. I knew that she was smoking ground-up mushroom powder. She used to send me to buy it from the old man, Buck Gussie, on Bengy Path. I said nothing to anyone because she said I mustn't. A lot of people used to go to the old man for cures if they were sick, and charms if they were in trouble, or to make them forget troubles.

Ma neither slept nor ate, and sat up all night chinking a nail on a glass bottle and smoking her pipe and shouting, 'I will make you fishers of men.' During the day, she cleaned up filth wherever she saw it and there was plenty about. We all cried because the other children teased us and the twins' friends no longer visited. They just covered their noses at us. The shame was like a stain on us. We sent for Ma's sister, Auntie Bet, a wonderful woman. She arrived with every possible liniment, potion, herb and medication she would need to take care of Ma. She wept when she saw Ma dancing without shame to the silent tunes in her head.

She said, 'I have come, sister, to take care of you in the name of our mother. Kneel down and let God direct us. Me to give. You to receive.'

Auntie Bet was longwinded in her praise of the Almighty.

We all knelt around Ma, and Auntie Bet said, 'Your children will shelter you. So be it!' Then she called down the spirits of all the women of our family who had passed over to God to help Ma.

And now Arnie had broken that pledge. I was very hurt and unhappy, but began to ease myself by finding my way around London and looking for rooms. But the ads mostly said, 'No blacks. No Irish. No dogs. No children'.

Thank the Lord I had consolation. After several months' frustrating delay, the divisional office had at last received my papers from home, and had assigned me to a school, to start in the new year. I could look forward to a class full of children eager to learn, or so I thought. Children from the West Indies had begun to come to England, and I guessed I would meet some of them at the school and teach them with love for our region in my heart.

My excitement mounted as the days passed. I imagined school as I had known it, teachers as I had known them, the children as children, with a childhood and a system structured and straightforward as the one under which I had been trained. I dreamt of doing well, of being patient and loving with the children in my charge. Having challenging work to look forward to made me much more tolerant with Trudi. I didn't react so aggressively when she called out, her voice thickened with a cold, 'Hello, Melda. Are you sulky today, or have you put it under the blanket?'

I showed her my teeth.

The snow fell — early that year, Arnie said. It was dense and impenetrable, saying subtle half-truths about whiteness: slippery, half-understood and unclean. I touched the snow, squeezed it and crunched it underfoot until I reached a famous bookshop in a London street. I had never before seen so many books in one place and was totally carried away. I bought one or two and proudly took them home.

Trudi and Arnie came in together. Trudi's face was red. She had been crying. It was usual in the yards for women to rush to the rescue of other women, but the barrier of colour was so complex between Trudi and me, there was no automatic reaction to her distress.

I decided to ignore her, and speak to Arnie.

'I went to Dillon's,' I said. 'It's a magical place — full of the most wonderful books on everything under the sun.'

Trudi glared at me. 'Who wants to hear about books? I am going to have a child and you are talking, "I saw books. Wonderful books!"'

I was so shocked, my voice came out in a squeak.

'A child! Arnie, you mad? A child with Trudi. A child who will hate its black half? Oh God! This will kill Pa and Ma.'

My mouth fell open. Arnie had made himself some tea which he poured into a saucer and slurped. I could hear it gurgling down. His stomach was empty as a gubby — full of sinful lust for Trudi, I supposed. She took the cup, sipped from it and said something about love and he smiled and hugged her.

'What will you do, Arnie?' I asked squeakily.

'I know what he will do. He will marry me! It does not concern your Pa and your Ma. Just we two. Me and Arnie.'

Arnie continued drinking his tea and looking with pleasure at Trudi.

'You must marry me, Arnie, or all my time will be used for nothing, I'm four months gone already.'

'Yes,' said Arnie. 'You want to get married? OK.' The way he spoke showed that he had decided to marry Trudi long before then.

She smiled triumphantly. 'See,' she said to me. 'It is so easy.

You must do the same. Get a man and say, "You will marry me." That is all you must do.'

I was too stunned for words. I went into my room and Trudi began to shout-sing 'Lili Marlene' in her language. It sounded as if she was tantalising me, but Arnie clapped and they sat talking and laughing until he went to work.

After that incident I had further doubts about Trudi. Arnie, however, trusted her and was kissy and kind to her. To my mind they were not at all suited; the processes that had led them to adulthood were different — too different. Arnie believed the whole world to be against him, and would only allow him a mite of anything — money, achievement, life, love, opportunity. Trudi, though, had extravagant dreams. Nothing was beyond her. She had life-skills that moved with her from country to country, job to job. She was in charge of Arnie and always would be. What she wanted of him I could not tell. She was intelligent, dominant and acquisitive. She would have a fine house, a good job, money in the bank, Arnie or no Arnie. With him, success would be harder to achieve, but manage it she would.

A month later they were married, a simple and quick wedding, which I did not attend. I showed no interest in the proceedings. Trudi's friend and her husband witnessed the event and the bride moved in with us. The downstairs people soon after disappeared, leaving the flat in a dreadful state, but I cleaned it and the landlord let me occupy it. Within the week I had moved downstairs at a greatly inflated rent.

I was no longer part of their lives. I had myself to think about and also about the wind, the snow and the weather as cold as an in-law's greeting. I bought a nice new mattress to sleep on, but the newly-weds did not notice.

A letter arrived from Mattie. She was delighted to hear of Arnie's marriage, and wanted to meet up with Trudi who, she hoped, looked like a film star.

'No,' I replied. 'She isn't a film star. She is the organ-grinder, and poor Arnie is the monkey, with frills round his senses.'

Meanwhile, I made myself more comfortable downstairs, and concentrated on locking out the comings, goings and performances of the newly-wed pair.

Arnie had developed a sprightliness of mind and movement, and a more contented look on his face, a look I hadn't seen since he used to count up the pennies he earned as 'Sunday chairboy', one of the boys who carried chairs for women dressed in their best clothes to sit on, when they visited the yards after Sunday church. He brought home much larger loaves of bread — already sliced up to prevent the argument over 'pulling at the bread and making it look so ugly'.

Trudi showed her special skills — knitting and sewing her layette. Arnie loved being looked after and, so wrapped up in his marriage, he pushed aside care and concern for me. He left me entirely on my own. But all was not smooth between the newly-weds. So often the lack of sophistication in the life Arnie had led back home showed through in his failure to keep Trudi happy with little considerations and surprises. She persisted in trying to reshape him. It was painful to listen to them.

'Arnie, I want some flowers. This time I buy it. Next time you learn to buy it for me.'

'You'll be so lucky. I ent no batty man messing about with flowers,' Arnie replied. The next week all hell broke loose when he forgot her birthday.

'Arnie, you did not get me the card for my birthday. You are a bad husband. Where are the flowers? You must remember.'

'Tell me why I have to remember your birthday. I don't remember mine, or my Ma's or my Pa's! Birthday! What's so special about the day you were born, Trudi? You are too vain.'

'You should think about people,' ordered Trudi.

'I haven't got time for birthdays. I have to think of the rent, the light, the heat, expense for your baby. I haven't got time for birthdays, for flowers, for nonsense. I'm going out.'

'Yes, run away. Run away from what is true.'

Arnie did not understand marriage, being a husband, or being a rock of support in anyone's life. He had learned to be a son, a brother, a carefree young man, a beach-roamer, a half-hearted, low-paid worker — but a substantial, upstanding husband was a very long way off his leanings. Marriage was like mending a hole in thatch. Something Trudi wanted done. So he did it. Responsibility — sustained and acknowledged — was, to my mind, beyond Arnie. I knew my brother. He hadn't married her. She, sad loss, had married him — led him to the Registry like a lamb to the slaughter.

The most irreparable loss for me was missing the opportunity to prepare for the wedding of my beloved brother. Where was the rejoicement and jubilation before the wedding? Where was the baking and icing the cake — blue for him and pink for her? Where was the beading to mark their adventures, pranks and excursions with others? Where was the singing, the drinking and the party-merriness? Most of all I missed the church service; the jovial assemblage and the speechifying with 'matrimonial felicitations' and wishes expressed in words longer than a long bamboo pole; the cutting of the cake, and the hugging up and embracing the other side.

I felt unhappy for days before the wedding. The whole thing was like a wake for the long-suffering dead. With all his getting, Arnie never got understanding. Ma, in her way, showed him the path. Pa put it before him. Mama Tat and Auntie Bet did their little bit for him. But the whole thing slipped out of his hands like a catch to a slap-dash cricketer. Now, talking to Arnie was like walking into a high wind, and dealing with Mrs Wife was like walking with a squall behind you — push-push, go-go, tumble. I didn't like any of it, so I sat down and propped up my sorrows, while taking comfort in the belief that, sure as God made morning, my brother Arnie had drunk from a poison-cup, rubbed his face with poison-ivy, and altogether made a bad mistake. There was nothing to do but swallow my spit and pray for a vision, showing how to rescue Arnie from the damnation of his choice. Oh God! The thought was fit to stifle me. I didn't know sound sleep for days. Fortunately, there was my teaching job to consider and plan for.

The calamity of Arnie and Trudi had strengthened my resolve and brought some of my most successful classmates to mind. While I had struggled against really heavy odds, some of them had gone overseas and returned with valued qualifications. I thought particularly of Clara McCase, with whom I used to study. She had no more brains in her head than a crapaud, but her father was rich and she had gone abroad to study medicine, while I struggled at home with poor children like myself. She never once missed the chance to tell me, 'Melda, I never cease to wonder how you so happy trying to throw stick so far.' She gave up her studies in the end and got married. She is now back at home.

Then there was Shelton, the skeleton, who used to hold us spellbound with the words in his mouth. He had swallowed a dictionary when he was a baby, and all of us believed in him. One day, when all the girls were kissing him, I kissed him too, and I felt my heart jump as never before. He had a sweetheart at home, but when he went away he did the same as Arnie. Everybody prepared for a wedding that never took place.

In the end I decided that being a teacher was a privilege, and was happy in the work which Mrs Penn chose for me. I would have liked to find out about the plants and flowers that I used to hide behind in my distress and pain. That, however, was not to be. No studying botany for me. Teaching was my only choice.

SECTION TWO

The earth sleeps on,
Its music dies,
Save for the gentle
Striding of my love.
I hear its echoes.
She approaches tenderly,
Stealthily retreats
Away from the door.
My perfect desire,
My Heart's paramour!
I yearn for her beauty
The night is at peace.

The burden of waiting
Merely echoes unease.

CHAPTER 3

Christmas had come and gone and my new working life was about to begin. I had been invited to a meeting at my new school on the day before term began. That morning I made myself ready and sat down to breakfast, unable to avoid hearing Arnie and Trudi in the upstairs flat.

Trudi was constantly sick and Arnie, dying to sleep after his nightshift, was as fretful as a baby with a sore backside.

'You mewing and squalling like a cat-woman!' he yelled. 'My mudda had five of us and she never carried on like dat!' He always reverted to creole under stress.

'I am not big and strong like your mother.'

'But you make more noise than a car engine, Trudi. You're stamping on my patience.'

'Oh Lord!' I said to myself. 'Where will it end?'

I had studied the route to my school, by bus and by train, and took care to arrive early. I was determined to do my best to make a good impression. I felt confidence sprinkled over with nerves, but calmed myself by knowing that all of us without exception were there to do our best. The thought of teaching always gave my heart that little push of pleasure. I felt certain I would be a teacher for ever. Just like Mrs Penn. A teacher in a million.

The headmaster was a short, slim man with an easy smile and a very firm handshake. He was also smartly dressed in a well-pressed suit and sober tie. There were more women than men on the staff; an Indian and myself were the only people from the 'sunny climes', as he put it.

We carved a circle with our handshakes and poured cups of tea before the formal meeting at which we received class registers, timetables and necessary information about the proper care of the children, about fire drill, medicals and lunchtime supervision. Much of this information was new to me, and I did not always pick up on the speech of those around me, but if I asked a question some of the others grew impatient. They expected me to know the system as well as they did.

I peered into what was to be my classroom. I would be in there with the children with no-one to ask for help. I would be responsible for the care and control of children I had never seen before, whose families I did not know, who probably had no love or respect for me. They knew my race only by gossip and folktales. I suddenly wanted to weep, for myself, for Arnie and for Trudi, and for the tragedies that would dog our lives all our days.

Then somebody knocked on the open door.

'I'm your 'elper, love. Rose. That's my name. Thought I'd say 'ello. I'm not due in till tomorrow but seeing as 'ow you're new, I thought I'd come. Anyfing want doing? I'll sharpen some pencils for you. Proper little tykes you 'ave in 'ere.'

She pulled out some keys, opened a cupboard and took out some pencils, which, using a desk sharpener, she went to work on. All the while she talked of the school, the families, the 'kids' as she called the children, and how the school had changed since 'you know, your people come'. She went on: 'You wanna be strict wiv 'em to start off wiv, and everyfing will be awlright. The black ones will take notice of you, but they don't listen to us. They call us mash, custards an' that.'

My head in a whirl, I went back to the assembly hall. The headmaster shook my hand again.

'Goodbye until tomorrow. I hope you will be happy here.'

'I am sure I will be, with you at the helm of this ship.'

'I'm not at the helm. Get to know my second-in-command at once! He does the legwork!'

Things were more puzzling than ever at these words. I watched him walk away, heard the crisp sound of his shoes and noticed the cheerful way he waved to everybody. There was something truly false about him.

When I left the school, I was not sure of my feelings about the job. They had changed in some extraordinary way and, try as hard as I could, I was unable to say why or how. Enigma was written all over the place.

Three letters were waiting for me when I arrived home. One from home, and two from New York. Pa had written and so had Mattie. The twins hardly ever wrote. Life held them in its clutches.

As I read Miss Lucretia's letter from home, a great overwhelming wave of anguish lifted me high into the air and threw me on my bed. Auntie Bet had died!

'Arnie!' I shouted. 'Come quick!'

Instead, the inquisitive Mistress Trudi came quick.

'Arnie, he is sleeping. What do you want with Arnie? Why must he be quick?'

'He must come! Shake him to wake him up. Tell him Auntie Bet is dead.'

'And where is this dead Auntie Bet? Arnie, he worked late. He is sleeping. I cannot tell him this.'

Arnie staggered out of bed and came down to my room, and we sat there sharing our misery and crying.

'What is this, Arnie? Why is this?'

Arnie gulped. 'My mudda, she had a nervous breakdown. Auntie Bet came and saved us. My mudda used to cry and say to my auntie, "Mammy, I want water," and my auntie gave her water. My mudda was a clean, proud woman who turned so mad she ate worms when her nerves dried to powder from loneliness and pressure. My auntie used to bite her lip to blood with sufferation for my mudda.'

'And where was the man of the house, your father? Where was this man?'

'Working in New York to buy us food. Auntie Bet got a doctor for my mudda. Auntie Bet saved her from the madhouse. My mudda was two people, one kind and gentle, the other like a barking, murderous creature. Auntie Bet saw the devil in Ma and spent her last cent to cure her. Auntie Bet came when we had no money for expensive doctors, and she nursed my ma with every care, looked after us, loved us, fed us.' Arnie stopped, exhausted, tears on his face. 'Auntie Bet defeat poverty, made us feel we rich, carried Ma on her back.'

'Well, that was her kindness. You did not ask it?' snapped the woman in blonde and blue.

How could she understand? A woman with history so much on her side. We were talking of naked, habitual poverty, not the war-created poverty that Trudi had known. Besides, she had run to her aunt in Switzerland while our Ma was raving mad, fighting her fears, wandering around troubled and confused, looking under dried bush and boscage for her long-dead mother. When we were in despair, God visited with Auntie Bet, who called herself our kinswoman, as in Bible times.

Miss Lucretia came to help us, and told Auntie Bet of an American preacher who had stopped in our country for a Salvation Crusade to make the word of God visible.

'He is a faith healer,' Miss Lucretia said. 'He has the power of God in his hands.'

Auntie Bet thought about it and decided to take Ma to the service.

'God move mysterious,' she said. She went to Mahamudeen and offered to hire his car for twice the price. He shook his head slowly.

'She is "going through", I can see that,' he said. 'But suppose she ca-ca or pee. There is my car done for by madness. I know madness is like fever — go anywhere. But not in my car!'

Auntie Bet did not beg, did not plead. She was far too proud. He was protecting his interests and rightly so. Money was his insanity. She tried Mr Sam. He too had a car, much older and noisier. He thought very hard and then, as if secreting something, with almost plaintive gestures, said in a matching voice, 'Suppose she show her lower self. Such people always show their lower self. Is madness, you know! Madness is a terrible thing.'

'All right,' she resolved. 'Jacqueline will still go! Lower self or no lower self.'

So Auntie Bet took thin, frail Ma on her back, in the true spirit of family, and started out. Arnie carried a chair for her to rest on. We plodded on, but before we had gone a little way, a car pulled up ahead of us. It was Mahamudeen.

'I am a Muslim. I must obey my religion. I went to school with her.' He jerked his head at Ma. 'Money is not everything. The Prophet, blessed be his name, place charity as a holy thing.'

He helped us with Ma, who was too ill to care about anything except her mutterings. As he drove, he talked of the time when his wife "went through".

'She had my fourth boy, Shamsudeen, and then her head turned to laughing loud, loud and cussing which is not good by our religion. She cried all night, all day. Then she built herself up with food and prayer. I believe in it. I feel ashamed that I refuse but that was devil-talk.'

The journey continued in silence, Auntie Bet quietly weeping and thanking God for his mercy. I didn't say anything. I didn't really understand God. Mr Mahamudeen stopped before a large hall as I recall.

'Mr Sam will come and pick you up. He owe me money. He will come. I will tell him to pay me by helping you all in the name of our blessed Prophet.'

We carried Ma to the open door, joining the queue that was building up. We could see into the hall, well-lit and containing a small platform, on which a table with a glass of water and a huge Bible awaited the preacher. A piano was half-hidden behind the curtains at the back of the stage.

The preacher strode on to the stage. He wore ordinary clothes which emphasised how tall he was.

'Let the brethren in,' he shouted.

And in we all came, a meek, pious, expectant, worried crowd, with hands clasped or folded. All dressed in best clothes — clean rags for some, stylish and expensive for others. The lady-singers, in spotless white, took their places and their voices rose in 'praiseful melody':

'Let us be humble together,
Safe in the love of our Saviour.
To Him uplifting in prayer
Desires known to our hearts.
We are the sick, the weak and the lame
We are the blind, the foolish, the maimed.
Give us your grace
Banish our pain!
Glory again and again!'

Ma was stirred. Her lips moved. She knew they were singing but was unsure of what she heard. Auntie Bet pushed her forward. Voices rose asking God to banish her pain and she, through some inner understanding, knelt down. We prayed. Everybody prayed for Ma. I took a sly look at Arnie. He was praying like mad. His lips moved rapidly.

'What are you saying?' I hissed at him. 'The Our Father?'

'No,' he whispered. 'Just sp-sp-sp-sp-sp-sp-sp-sp like the big people.'

I nudged him with my elbow and shut him up.

The preacher now had his hands on Ma's head. Ma screamed as if in great pain.

'Confess! Feel the power! Feel the need! Confess!'

'I won't do it no more!' Ma bleated. 'My cup of abomination is full.'

'What won't you do no more?'

'Smoke the powder, mushroom-powder. I won't no more.'

Ma talked of how she had found the mushroom we called jumbie-umbrella, and the man in the hut had long ago told her it was medicine. She had found it again since Pa had gone and now it had turned on her, and cursed her senses.

'I am in darkness. Help me move to light. I can see beautiful lights! Hear devil voices calling, calling.' She fell in a whimpering heap at the pastor's feet, her face washed over with pain and then with peace.

The singing rose again.

'Cleansed! Cleansed in the name of the Saviour.
Cleansed! Cleansed in the name of the Lord.
Cleansed is our mother, our sister.
Gone are those seeds that were bitter,
Cleansed through the Saviour's love.'

The singing continued till Ma rose up and walked away. They gave us back our Ma, and she returned to her chair renewed in strength. She slept soundly all the way home and began to speak the next day to her many visitors. Ma was better than she had ever been in recent times.

The pastor also visited us to give Ma extra blessing. He blessed the house, and the devil of the psychedelic mushroom was gone, 'burnt alive by the preacher's might'. Ma ate and talked, joked and smiled. She knew happiness again.

And now Auntie Bet had died, she who had lived in service to the yards and faithful service to us.

'You look as if you are dreaming,' Trudi said abruptly. 'Now, Arnie, you must go back to bed and forget this dead Bet.'

'Why don't you shut your mouth?' I snapped.

I went to my own flat, certain that Ma and Pa would return home to bury Auntie Bet, who had no use for men, and for many years had lived in sisterhood with women. Healing, helping, sewing, giving of her time, her skills and her boundless love.

'Men,' she had said, 'put brakes on women. They put training-strings on them.' She had a head working to protect her woman's body from blows, beatings and misuse. I lay on my bed bringing her and the yards back to life until a sharp voice intruded.

'Are you not yet asleep?' Trudi demanded through a crack in my door, as she let Arnie out to begin his all-night shift.

'Listen to me. Your aunt was old and powerless and now she is dead. Is that not good? Why must she have extra from this life?'

I did not reply. But she ran on. 'A bomb fell on our house. My father, my mother and my sister did not even get to say thank you for killing us. I run away. Thirteen, I was. I see this black man. I say, "Come. I will help you". I need always to rescue people, because I could not rescue my loving people.'

She had said her piece. Now she would sleep. I did not believe her. Where could she find a black man waiting for help, running from Germans? Why should she want to rescue my brother?

I kept imagining the wake for Auntie Bet, the lovely hymns, and I even hummed 'Abide with me', which she was singing the last time I saw her.

After Ma had got over her illness, Auntie Bet wrote to Pa and he at once sent tickets (paid for, it turned out, with money borrowed from his cousin Dorian) for all of us to come to him. But Ma decided to remain at home until I finished my studies. She didn't want America. It was too far from the yards — too far from her roots. She talked with Mama Tat about her problems, and she promised to be company with her come what may. So Ma sent Flora and Florizel, much too eager for life, with Mattie and Jacko to Pa, but he really wanted her to come too.

She said she would go to him as soon as my exams were done. Now Ma talked of Pa, whom she called Henry, saying what a nice man he was, and what a fine tenor voice he once had, and how he used to sing 'Bless This House' to her. Arnie had tried to join the Army, lying about his age, but they saw through him and he too stayed at home looking after Ma, and working on the boat with Mr Walker.

Auntie Bet had come to see the children off, and sent guava cheese and cassava bread for Pa in New York. She hugged and kissed each child while Ma, still conscious of having poor authority over us, stretched out a stiff hand of goodbye. Auntie Bet blessed the travellers and then their journey, with a prayer that lasted a full ten minutes. Then she boarded the bus back home, shouting as she waved, 'Hard work and manners maketh man.' I never saw her in the flesh again although we frequently exchanged messages.

Arnie had saved up the money he earned fishing and suddenly decided to go to London because even 'worse-up' people were going. He went to say goodbye to Auntie Bet and left with his share of her 'etceteras'. I was now alone with Ma and we became quite close, although neither of us ever forgot that she was not my birth-mother. I wondered what my own parents were like, but, knowing that 'Speech is silver', I was careful to conceal my curiosity and never asked her any questions. One day, though, she told me that Pa was indeed my father, but that he and her sister showed her hell.

We were dreadfully lonely for the others, especially when we began to be pestered by Mr Walker, father of Tim. He would pass round and talk with Ma, till Mama Tat or one of the other women appeared, and cause him to scuttle off like a lizard through the grass to his house. Sometimes he would walk along the lanes and strike up conversations with young girls. He was a vulgar old man who forgot he was a father and husband and would offer young girls good money to 'start them off'. He believed virgins had good oil in their lamps, and would bring him luck and make him rich. He was not a pleasure to see. His belly floated out before him, showing both the beer and the fat, while his face portrayed the worst features of the races which he contained. Watching his behaviour was like eating a very unpalatable meal. It left a bitter taste in my mouth and a stinging in my throat. If I was within a foot of him, with no one else in sight, his fingers always seemed ready to jump and grab me.

'You pretend you don' love me! I have money in the bank.' The words always came out in a hoarse whisper as he leered and grinned at me through his tobacco-stained teeth. The man was not joking.

Yes, Grandfather, to put you in a coffin, I thought. But I never spoke out, preferring to ignore him and run off. In stressful situations my voice usually disappeared, and bitter memories crept out from all the corners of my mind, wrapping me round and round the way a spider wraps its prey.

Yet there was a part of me that was fortified against attack, held like a little shoot in hope and ambition. None could touch that place, by word or deed. Under pressure, its light flickered a little, but never went out. That part of me was at the centre of my certainty. I knew I would be somebody and do something worthwhile in life. I often met those people who lived in my mind, people whose touch I felt on my cheek and on my arm. I called them my mind-ghosts and was sure that they were my ancestors, whom Auntie Bet so often called up in prayer. My protectors, they brought me ideas, principles and truth. The desire to persevere, and to try things made me able to forgive and accept weakness in others and to resist evil wherever its thorns appeared. Mr Walker and his antics did the worst they could do. They made me hurry down the lane, open the door, my breath in a flurry — a great turbulence in my brain. But I did not tell Ma. I often wondered why I did not. Was it because I saw her as ineffectual, or did that attention do something for the vanities of the woman in me?

I would shake my head at those thoughts and decide that to be a proper woman I had to suffer. I tried to pray for Mr Walker, but could never move beyond 'Oh God' and then all his wild words would come pouring over me again. I was like the women in the yards — they went on about their unjust treatment, but did nothing to change it. They expected conditions and situations to change of themselves, so they left matters to God, while they wept and howled to one another, and their men did worse each day. After thoughts like those, I finally went to bed, asking myself why should I worry. How many times did anyone pass through this life? Once and only once. There is never time for rehearsal.

Ma had lain down to reduce the effects of rum which she drank from a little glass before her bedtime. I lay there listening to the sounds minted by the darkness and its creatures, grateful that faith and love and, indeed, hope had returned to our house, and that Pa had sent us a torch by which we could give meaning to the sounds and silences of the night.

I fell into a troubled sleep. Suddenly something stirred and I woke with a start. A rough hand landed over my mouth, snuffing out my cries. I reached for the torch but it fell with a clatter to the floor. Another hand grabbed my breasts with crude ferocity, and a ponderous, sweaty paunch pushed against my hand. Ma appeared, the torch in one hand, in the other a short stick that was always kept close to her pillow. She worked this vigorously upon the apparition which, in the dim light of the torch, turned into the incoherent Mr Walker, driven towards my bed by his lechery. He was smiling as he let go of me.

'Holler for help,' said Ma. 'Holler! Open the window.'

Footsteps hurried towards us — men and women eager to catch a thief. Mr Walker stood before them, his trousers in disorder. The men, ashamed of being men, and the women, of being women, lowered their eyes.

'Well,' said Soldier Boy, 'Why you come, Mr Walker?'

'He too drunk,' said Scoutie McCaul. 'Rum is responsible. All his generation was drunkards. He too drunk to answer questions.'

'Don't talk about his generation. They dead and gone. His Pa used to be decent to us every Christmas. Answer the question. Why you come?'

My sobs came in a gush as the talk flowed, then in full flood.

'You forgetting the girl. You forgetting the poor, pained girl. It worse dan if he cut her. The red dog!'

'His mouth is dirty. He talks about women even on a Sunday.'

'He is not respectable. He is a dog.'

Ma took me into her room and offered me a chamber pot of hot water to kill any germs that accidentally had jumped on me.

'He can give you a shock. Bet believe in hot water,' she whispered confidentially. 'Thank God, Walker only thought bad!'

Not knowing what to do with a male deviant, the men drifted back to bed, leaving Mr Walker sprawled half asleep on the floor, rolling his head from side to side. Had he been a woman, he would have been soundly beaten by the eager men.

'Call his wife,' suggested Mama Tat, as she stroked her crumpled face.

'Ha ha!' laughed the culprit. 'She's a holy woman. I'll show her my gun. She has not seen it in years.'

'Which gun?' asked Baiy-Baiy Daly.

'This,' said Mr Walker, pointing to himself.

'You stupid? You can't even frighten a god-bird with that! Don't be so clownish,' snapped Mama Tat.

By now, everyone had turned over the talk for long enough. The women dragged Mr Walker outside and poured cold water over him. Bucket after bucket was poured over him until, looking like a fledgling that had fallen out of the nest, he stumbled off into the darkness.

I sat down, crying with disappointment that his intentions had been lost in the confused discussion. My tears fell drop by drop upon the cat sitting on my lap.

'Don't wet up the poor kyat,' snapped Ma.

'Poor kyat! What about poor me?' I snapped back.

'This is an "of course" situation,' said Miss Lucretia. 'He didn't do nuttin' and yet he frighten the girl enough to make her barren later on.'

An "of course" situation is one which is clear for all to see beyond a doubt.

Miss Maybelle served coffee, while Miss Daisie asked, 'Whose fault made Mr Walker so disrespectable?'

'Is the mudda fault!'

'The mudda fault!' came a chorus of voices. 'Because we born them?'

'No! How we raise them. We raise them slack.'

My eyes raced round the group, all contrasting shades of brown that ran into the darkest skin of Miss April. Suddenly she burst out, 'I was an ugly one. Blackest of all. My mudda never run out of cuss for me. She run out of kindness, sympathy, understanding, but never out of cuss. She call me every name from fish-eye to liver-lip. I never care.'

'You can't blame you' mudda. Who can say they prefer a black-skin? Only a reckless person. Black mean poor, mean hungry, mean drinking stinking water. Working in the trash.'

'Don't talk rubbish. Besides, we ent talking about you' mudda, we talkin' about that ole man an this girl here. You blame the girl?'

'Of course, I don't blame that girl!'

'This is an "of course" situation,' said Daisie, who had started the discussion. 'The girl in her bed where she put herself. And then this covetous man come. It is a clear situation. They think what they have is a fairy wand. They wave it over you. And you done dead for them,' said Daisie, with passion like gravel in her voice.

'Yes, this world should be full of women. You see *we* with sticks, weapons, guns, knives, ropes, cord or whatever?' agreed Lucretia.

Afterwards, I remained in a dream state, imagining that Mr Walker crept with me every step of the way — getting into my eyes like sand. There was no place to hide as we were on a desolate beach with the raging sea beyond. He caught up with me and I felt his weight, inhaled his foul breath, my arms confined, my voice frozen by humiliation and terror.

A year or so later, my night terrors stopped when Mrs Walker died of breast cancer. She had been desperately ill for a long time. Her illness had turned her husband into a rampant tiger — which would have been reasonable if he hadn't dug his claws into someone who loathed him.

We watched the pitiful cortège, and people out of habit crossed themselves. Mr Walker's grief had rehabilitated him and he was offered sympathy.

Soon after, Pa returned from America to fetch Ma. This time, persuaded that she was needed there and I would cope at home, she acquiesced and went on her own long journey across the seas. I went to live with Mrs Penn, where I could pursue my studies in peace. I used to look out from the window of my room to our house, now sold to other people, and think of the unscripted parts I had been pushed into playing there.

Suddenly, I realised that my life had taught me to love women, but left me ignorant of men. I had never seen Pa and Ma sharing and tolerating each other's weaknesses, and discussing things with love and tender talk. If things went wrong, Ma sulked, or was cruel to us, or complained to Mama Tat about Pa, or about us. There was never any real wish for change. Pa went off to work with the men, worked when he could, lay in the hammock when he had no work, or threatened to go away. At the age of twenty-five, I knew nothing about making a relationship with a man which could grow in strength, flourish and endure. Like all the women I knew, I dismissed everything I could not understand about men as aberrations or idiosyncrasies or 'jes' man's ways' — like the women in the yards. Miss Daisie always said, 'People learn everything through experience.' I had none.

I heard Arnie come in from his shift and, around half-past seven, Trudi, her belly now visibly swelling, brought me tea.

'Here you are,' she said. 'Your auntie still dead. From now on she is finished. Caput. Like my father.'

Trudi was not of the world I knew. She was different to us in every way — made of flesh over stone. The way she threw words at me spoke for itself.

It was the first day of term. I dressed in my skirt and twinset and took the bus and train to the school. I was sorry I did not see Arnie before I left for work. He was the only link with my past, my beliefs and the values that I had absorbed at home and in the yards. I had learned to notice things and then to follow up with concern and action. I had taken to heart the lessons learned in a black family that was poor but decent. All of them I carried with me to sprinkle over what life would give me.

Ma and Pa would be going home to bury Auntie Bet. She had left them her house for their old age. I was happy to start teaching.

CHAPTER 4

It was my first day in an English school. I entered the gate and made my way through the yard where black children inter-mingled with white ones. When the bell rang, the children ploughed into the classrooms and continued the rough-and-tumble of the playground. School, or being at school, had no special meaning for them. They were in charge.

When I stood in front of my class, a voice said, 'Are you our teacher?'

I nodded. Then the child said to the one beside him, 'She *is* our teacher.'

Another voice said, 'Look at her! Yuck!'

'I am Miss Hayley,' I said. 'I come from the West Indies like some of you here. Who is from the West Indies?'

The entire class raised their hands and a child said, 'I'm going there. I will go with my friend.'

I called the register and they melted into laughter at the way I pronounced their names. The worst was over and we sailed into open water. They practised writing, while Rose, the helper, pointed out the 'roughs' and the 'lawbreakers'.

The difference between these children and those I had taught at home was enormous. These children chose when to obey, when to listen, or when to co-operate. It was impossible to get them to sit still. The black children I had taught at home did not shout at, challenge or disobey any teacher. I was so preoccupied with controlling these, so fully extended in my skills as a teacher, that I forgot milk-time until a voice beside me said, 'You're hopeless. You forgot our milk.'

At the word 'milk', they pushed whatever they were using aside and dived for the bottles. None of my class was seven years old as yet. I wondered what they'd be like at ten.

After the break, the head arrived in my class.

'Well,' he said. 'How are you coping so far?'

'They are unruly,' I replied. 'They don't seem to see me.'

'We select them at six. And you've got the rejects. Nobody else wanted them. They are mostly your own kind.'

I could not believe my ears.

'I'm leaving here soon,' he continued. 'I don't like change. I don't like what is happening here. We had a good record here. Now, for a cup of tea!'

Discipline varied from teacher to teacher. Some staff were like myself, preoccupied with trying to bring shape to the working day. Others were more pragmatic or even laissez-faire. It was a school where children constantly called each other insulting names, but then one of the teachers had nicknamed a black child 'Snowy'.

There were some who cared. 'Keep it formal for as long as it takes. This lot rule their parents and try it on us,' one old teacher advised.

When I returned to the class, I increased my strictness by twenty points. The children had to co-operate or miss play. They were very angry and talked about bringing their dads to 'biff' me and even about going 'on strike'. Each day I kept to the same strict format and they began to accept that I was in charge.

The West Indian parents weren't sure about me. Like their children, I had only just arrived and in their eyes was a 'learner' who could not help their children's progress. Those children who felt they weren't indulged or given their own way cried easily and accused me of 'hating' them. I explained that I was there to teach them, and that I did not like them enough to hate them. I was interested only in their work, and some of them did so little and fussed so much.

What I found most difficult was the dislike of change shown by the staff. They saw all foreigners, whatever their age or education, as uncivilised. To be civilised was to speak English and, more importantly, to be English. It was also no fun working as a new member of staff under a headmaster who disliked being 'used by parents, the staff and the local authority'. The headmaster was sure of his identity and careful of his dignity. He was English and conservative and, by rights, England was for the English. He expressed his opinions candidly. To him, foreign children, no matter how able, blighted the system.

Some teachers could cope with the white working classes and their concerns, but not with the problems of immigrants. These newly-arrived children were co-operative and trusting — until they realised that nothing they did could truly please their teachers. It was as if they were expected to change their culture on the way to school each day, so the teachers could approve of them. Most teachers served only an English meal and if the children could not enjoy it, that was their fault. There were, though, a few teachers who understood that many of these children were culture-shocked. Where there was sympathetic support, it was surprising how quickly the children picked up English and the peculiarities of the culture.

As the days flowed by, I went home drained, and beaten down by the childminding that passed for teaching. The school was either a battleground or a playground as the day progressed, and at times a horror show. How could the children grow in competence, when there was no planning of what they should learn, when there was no awareness of the problems of adjustment that many children faced, or any understanding of why some children resented what called for sustained effort? In some cases, we were asking children for skills they did not have — especially social skills.

I asked to see the head. He couldn't spare the time.

'You should get to know my second-in-command ASAP,' he said.

I racked my brain wondering what ASAP meant, until, defeated, I asked a colleague.

'That's shorthand for "as soon as possible",' she replied. 'You people take the cake. Fancy not knowing a thing like that!'

Things came to a head when money was taken from my purse. Everybody was sure that the culprit was Georgie Sharpe. He was a boy who seemed to have little interest in learning. He had experienced the traumatic childminding common at the time. His file was supposed to be private, but I was urged to read it.

'He takes dinner money off the children,' the deputy head confided. 'The little tea leaf. I'll give him a transfer one of these days. I'll transfer him to our neighbours.' He giggled nervously. 'Our neighbours' was a school close by.

I asked Georgie about the money.

'I never done it,' he replied, out of habit.

Two days later, Mrs Sharpe swaggered into the class. She hesitated a little before jerking her head in the direction of her son and accused him of having stolen ten bob. 'When I asked the little bastard where he got it from, he said out of your purse. Do me a favour. Put your purse where the kids can't get at it. It's placing temptation on them.'

'If things don't belong to Georgie, he should leave them alone, like a decent Christian child.'

'Oh yeah,' she said. 'Oh yeah!' She gathered her saliva together and spat at me. 'We are Church of England. Don't you dare tell my kid what he ought to do.'

I seized her hand and began dragging her to the staffroom, where the deputy head was having coffee. She kicked me, and I gave her a stinging smack which quickly brought her to her senses. Up to that point I had never touched white. I never even touched the children. I couldn't do it.

'I'll summons you...' she yelled. 'I'll summons you for assault.' Suddenly she reached over and wiped away her spit from my clothes. I was angry almost to convulsions. I prayed to God to turn me away from murder.

By the time the Head came down she denied spitting at me, shouting, 'Show me where I spat! Show me!'

Later, the divisional officer sympathised, but there was nothing could be done for lack of evidence. Though the helper, Rose, had seen everything that had taken place in the room, she refused to be a witness for me, insisting that she'd rather not 'get mixed up'. I could not believe my ears. Staff explained it by saying, 'Rose isn't teaching staff', but I still could not make sense of it. Later, however, Rose explained that she lived in the same block of flats as my assailant and her life would have been hell. That I did understand.

I was slowly learning new ways of looking at life, of filtering reactions — mine as well as others. It was not only race and colour, but the way people reached conclusions about others that caused conflict. So much at school made me bristle. Trying to 'read' my colleagues was a particular burden. I could read the face and body language of people back home, could recognise joy, sorrow, pleasure and welcome. Now, whatever were the words said, I could not tell what people really meant. I asked to be sent to another school, and before too long I was stifling my pain, smiling at my prospects and chancing my luck again.

The new school had been built shortly after the war, but while the building was fairly new, the teachers were in an older tradition, trained years before the war and committed to helping the children make progress and grow in self-respect. It was a privilege, they said, to be allowed to work with growing young minds. They concentrated on what children were expected to know at every stage and made sure they did. They respected the fact that children were individuals, but then went on to demand effort, hard work and commitment from all of them.

It was so similar to Mrs Penn's school that I settled in quickly. The children were keen to learn, to collect credits for their work and to be first in the next test. Competition was a game to them. They disliked being helped and struggled with their work until they succeeded in mastering it. They were eager to hear of other countries and other peoples, the crops they grew, the products they manufactured, and other important things about them.

There was, though, one little African girl who felt bothered by the talk of difference. *She* had not come from Africa. *She* had found herself on the train and *she* was white. She was the same as her white friends, Sarah and Emily and Sally. She held herself together by this denial.

'Don't you want to come from Africa? I asked.

'No. I wouldn't have my toys, my mum and my dad' (her foster parents) 'or my clothes. None of them are in Africa.'

At first, no-one on the staff was openly hostile to me. Their questions seemed genuine if not very welcoming.

'What could you possibly do for this country?'

'Why not help your own country?'

These were fair questions, and I think that some of them really wanted to understand, but I did not try to justify my presence in England as a teacher or in any other way. I simply followed my professional instincts and tried to do a good job. I was just beginning to feel secure when the headmaster was promoted to a bigger school and a new headmistress arrived. From the very first moment she talked of 'our children being overwhelmed or held back'. She used emotive words cleverly and soon collected a clique of followers among the staff.

I resolved that despite everything I would go on working in Britain, but that heaven must spare me the shame of dying past work-age in this country.

I changed my mind when I saw what happened to another

teacher. She was addicted to touching the children and moving them where she wanted them.

'Why do you touch the children? They aren't chess pieces. Tell them what you want them to do! Use words!' the Head ordered, her voice crackling like corn over fire. The woman shrugged and walked away. Hurrying after her, the Head told her, as crossly as she could, and within earshot of others: 'Go to the Divisional Office. Say what you like about me but do not come back here.' The woman wept unashamedly. Nobody moved to comfort her. Nobody saw or heard.

I decided not to wait for my turn to taste the new head's bigotry or methods of intimidation. It was not an easy decision to take. Gone would be my dreams of developing in the profession for which I had so assiduously trained. I felt quite guilty, too, about my 'desertion'. I had specialised as a teacher of reading, and my skills would be unused and lost to the scores of children who could not read and who sorely needed them. I knew, too, that the few black children would later be quietly persecuted out of the school, and their parents, already powerless, would be rendered even more so.

So, just when it seemed for a moment that things were going right for me at last, they fell apart. Perhaps God, Fate and Life were beckoning me in other directions. I told Arnie of my predicament and he, of course, told Trudi. They communicated through the medium of other people's miseries, especially mine. Trudi came downstairs to sympathise.

'Do not worry about these pigs! They are the same as the bad people who dropped a bomb on so serious a man as my father, Helmut. Often, I can kill these people.'

She held her hand like a flower on top of her very large, very round belly. The scraggy blonde hair hung limply around her face. The anger she felt at the death of her father was still intense. I felt a lump in my throat.

'Not long from now you'll be a mother. Think about that. Don't worry about me.'

'But you must get a job. It will be a worry for Arnie and me.'

'Don't worry about me. I'll get a job soon.'

That same night, little Stefan, Arnie's son and my nephew, weighed in at six pounds and ten ounces. If Arnie was happy, there was not the slightest show of it in his face, except for the fact that he left work in a hurry and went to the hospital with flour on his hands. I burst out laughing as I imagined the scene. Trudi's voice, clear as a bell, came to me.

'Arnie! Your hands! What is this on your hands? They are so white. You have to come to show your bakery to the baby. You are so lazy. You did not wash.'

A month or so after I left the school, I received a kindly letter from the oldest member of staff, encouraging me to continue teaching. 'The children will be the losers, for you are a committed teacher of young children.' She was a woman with a sparkling vision and British in the best tradition. She was all for fairness and was without prejudice. She believed in people who understood justice. Sadly, I could not reply to her letter. She had omitted her address, and it was chancy sending letters to the school.

In the space of six months of teaching, I had begun to understand how the class to which you belonged fitted you into the jaws of the system. West Indians, being thought of as foreigners, were condemned always to stand on the fringes. Ma and Pa, who believed in Queen, Country and Empire, would not have been able to understand that those of us who dared to claim our colonial inheritance had to plead or even grovel for a hearing.

My money, Mrs Penn's generous bequest, was being whittled away as if by a reckless wood carver. But I would not lose heart. I would enjoy a self-imposed holiday and then test the water once more. Each day, through some gentle memory, some unfailing truth, I recalled Mrs Penn.

But trying to read quietly in my room, I was tortured by the sound of Trudi's voice. She spoke compulsively to her baby, like a three-year-old at dolly-play. He was never at peace, and was so conditioned to the sound of her voice that, when she stopped talking, he jumped awake, screaming for more. There was never a moment when he wasn't being handled, washed, dressed, kissed and cuddled. Of course, Arnie was not reared to such caperings, and soon got fed up with them and became indifferent. They quarrelled at least once a day.

My spirits, though, were lifted when Mattie wrote to say she would arrive in a month. I was delighted and allowed my heart to rush into indulgent thoughts of every kind. In my imagination I saw her, still a little child, young and tender, thumb in mouth, open-eyed to the wonders of life, untouched by adult guile.

The time until she came passed slowly. Arnie's and my impatience did not please Trudi who demanded, 'Who is this Mattie? I will not be here when she comes. I will go home with my Stefan.'

'Did Arnie play any part in getting Stefan?'

'You mean in the manufacture of Stefan? You must not ask that. It is not decent to ask such things. Now I must go out. I want to buy for Stefan a little — how do you say it? — a pottie.'

'What! So soon? He's barely three months old. Just muscle and soft bone.'

'You do not know about these things. Nor do you know school things.'

'I know he'll have his whole life to sit on a pot and it's no use starting him at this time.'

'Well, then, I will not buy the pot.'

But she did, all the same. She kept it hidden away until one day she said, as if I would be enchanted by the news, 'Stefan has got a present.'

'Good. He is lucky — a lucky baby. Someone came to see him?'

'No, the present is from me, his mutti. What is better than the present from his mother?'

'What is it?' I steeled myself to ask. 'Show me.'

With a flourish, she produced the pot. 'Now he will learn.'

'Yes, of course.'

Later than evening Arnie came home and, while he was eating, was enthusiastically introduced to the pot.

'I don't want to hear about that when I am eating, Trudi.'

'Why? It is empty. There is nothing in it.'

'Well, put it where people go to do pots.' He pulled a disgusted face and thought for a long while. Then the dam inside him burst.

'Trudi, why you making a "batty-man" of my son? Grow him up hard. Instead you wrap him up in cotton wool. You will repent. The boy is like a Sunday-monkey. You always dressing him like a girl—an auntie-man. He'll be a sissy-man. A wife-man wearing powder.'

He pushed the food aside. The baby began to cry. Anxiously, I walked a little way downstairs.

'See your big throat. It is terrible, your big throat!' Trudi screamed at Arnie. 'You would scare elephants.'

The baby continued to scream.

'Oh God, this is too much! This is torment. Oh God, I going to sleep at my sister!' Arnie yelled. 'You making me take God name in vain!'

'You going to sleep with her! That is a sin! What about me, your wife?'

'What the hell you talkin' 'bout, woman? You mad-talkin' witch!'

He slapped her hard. She and the baby both shrieked again. She took a jug and threw it at Arnie. It shattered at his feet.

'You devil! You're nothing but a devil, like all your race! All of you! My foreparents had a whip on their backs. Now I have you. You beating me till I shout God's name, you slave-driver. Torturer!'

I put on my hat and coat and went out. I sat in the park and watched the children playing and looked at the flowers which were colourful, but never as bright as those I had left behind at home.

When I returned, peace had been declared. Arnie had gone back to work and Trudi talked to her son.

'Your papa, he is a good man. A good child, like you. What will you be when you grow up, eh? A fine man? You look like Arnie, your papa. Read books and know better than he. You are my son. Your mother is called Trudi and you are welcome to her heart!'

'Trudi,' I said. 'You did not hear what Arnie said. He sleeps in my little room to get peace. Think on that. He does not sleep on or with me.'

'Thank you for telling me your secrets.'

Her voice seemed to become the voice of the parrot owned by the old Amerindian who sold Ma medicines. The bird used to come close to the window and then, in a mysterious manner, say, 'T'anks for buying. Go away. Go away.' This used to make me stop in my tracks, glower at the bird and conduct the business as quickly as I could, thinking all the while I had come face to face with a jumbie. If I had Mattie with me, I would run with her on my back along the overgrown path, no longer worried about stepping on snakes.

SECTION THREE

The vision of a loved one
Materialises out of longing;
Love's seeds show in tender shoot;
Spirits soar,
Blessing stars
And melon moon in praise
For Youth's becoming.
Celebrations!
Green-limbed moments
Dash headlong
And fancy free
To form resistant memory.
The past was ours.
The future theirs.
*'Tis **now** that scares!*

CHAPTER 5

Mattie arrived, a pretty girl, but without the pastel-shaded innocence which had marked her every word and gesture before she moved to America. There was now an edge to her voice, and her eyes contained a harsh, tight darkness to which light came slowly. Slim, slightly built, narrow-hipped and long-legged, Mattie could never be described as other than striking; yet the charm for which the yard women had loved her had become self-interested. No longer could she be kept 'little' by remarking on her tidiness, her neatness or her manners. She was eighteen and grown-up. She spoke with the authority of all kinds of free-ranging experience. No more neat, tidy, conventional clothes — Bermuda shorts, sweaters and flared jackets were what she wore under her coat.

'How's school?' I asked the remains of the little baby sister I had often carried on my back.

'OK, though sometimes my goals ran away before I could take hold. I missed too much school back home. I have a part-time job. If they make it full time, I'll quit school. I hated school at first. The kids teased me about the way I talked and how I dressed. They still do. So I'll quit.'

'Ma and Pa say you could?'

'They're old and rheumaticky now. Glad for all the help they can get. They don't know how American kids carry on. They don't care for us. Black on black is good fun.'

'Don't you all pull together for Ma and Pa? The twins, Jacko and you? I know Arnie sends money and I do regularly. Ma and Pa are our responsibility. Not the government, not the church — ours.'

'Who can rely on the twins? They don't call themselves Flora and Florizel no more. Call themselves Mona and Lisa after some dumb picture in Paris. Mona Lisa. They're crazy. Jacko runs a taxi. Making money has him by the neck. He's more moody than the tides back home.'

She chewed her gum with a cool detachment, though its size suggested dumplings in her mouth. I watched her as she chewed, her thoughts darting from place to place and thing to thing like flies. I admired the skill with which she folded and caressed her clothes. They meant something special to her. I remembered what Mrs Penn had said. We valued clothes because in slavery clothes were given as a reward and thereby became a part of our identity. To naked Africans they meant power and civilisation. As we walked to the shop, I watched her swaying walk that said, 'Beware! Here I come!'

'The twins buy a lot of things and pass them on. What I can't wear, I sell to friends,' she said. 'You got a map of London? Tomorrow I'll go visit Buckingham Castle where the Queen lives. If you don't have a map, I'll buy one.'

'Mattie,' I said hugging her. 'You've grown up and I am glad you're here. Not Castle! Palace.'

'It makes no difference. You know what I mean.'

We sat and talked of old times, and life in New York.

'Pa learned plumbing and he gets work. In the summer, he sells papers. We manage. The twins, they do good dancing at the Cob Club. They're good. They going to be stars one day. Well, they say so all the time. Florizel is an A-class tap dancer. They both go around with dancers. They do good.'

'You in love, Mattie? Boys like you?'

'They do, too. But they no good. Gambling, dropping out of school. There was this boy called Troy, but he ain't no way near me now. I don't like what his brother Calvin done.'

'What?'

'He was locked up and lost a great deal of money in a game in prison to a guy named Horse-Neck. When Horse-Neck discharged he parked on Calvin's wife 'cause Calvin gave him permission to use her for debt. Troy thought that was real funny. So I heaved him out of my window.'

'Well, how's the asthma?'

'Comes and goes! In winter we ain't friends. Pa sits by me, holds my hands. I'll never forget how he stood in half a ton of mud digging a grave so he could get money to buy a doll with gold hair, blue eyes, party clothes and shoes. Told me the other day.'

'I remember. He was covered with mud. He even had it on his hat. Poor Pa. An angel if ever there was one.'

'I go along half-way with that. But you know, once Ma had us, Pa thought that all she ever needed was food. He didn't know how to give her anything else, like affection, appreciation and love.'

I heard the key in the lock and was immediately covered in goose-flesh. Trudi and Stefan, I thought rapidly. Poor little wrapped-up and powdered thing. But in fact it was our tired, persecuted brother. A slow fire seemed to be burning inside him. When, however, he saw Mattie, a smile lit up his face. His fingers, at first set in the mode of kneading dough, relaxed into the softest of touches.

'Sweet-sister, Mattie! God bless this day!'

He hugged us and for a moment the thread of family wound itself firmly around us, binding us together invisibly, yet truly. For a moment, the years — ragged, relentless and numerous — passed before our eyes, all our eyes, but we did not speak, did not smile or laugh. We stood hand-in-hand looking back, inch by deprived and impoverished inch, along the years we called the past.

Then Arnie said, 'Tell me about Pa.'

'What's to tell? He will put the last crumb of bread in Ma's mouth. Give her the only slice of cake, give her the last cent. Pa don't want nothing for himself. He got no self. He only got soul.'

'H'm,' said Arnie. 'I have to remember his patience every day. I married, you know. Not much of a wedding. She's OK, but when I look at my life, is like a rope. She on one end, I on the other and poor little Stefan in the middle.'

'Stefan! What kind of a name is that?'

'Is her language for Stephen.'

Soon after, Trudi returned with Stefan and was introduced to Mattie. Stefan moved his eyes from face to face and, seeing a stranger, began to fuss and cry in his scraping, bottom-of-the-bottle-voice. For a small baby he had a big voice.

We sat down to a meal I had made of rice and stewed peas, with spicy, fried cod. It was a fresh, homely dish. Trudi did not say much.

Arnie was so happy to have Mattie close that we three became another family. Trudi, feeling excluded, ignored us unless she had to do otherwise, though she constantly called upon Arnie to perform chores.

'The baby, he has colic. Bring me the hot water bottle.'

'I'll do it just now.'

'What is this just now? What is just now? Do it now.'

Arnie would carry on talking to Mattie, and for peace I would help Trudi. She either grudgingly accepted my help or rudely said, 'Oh, I can do it. Go and make a nasty bell with your voice.'

Being young, Mattie had no patience with Trudi, and the stress brought on her asthma.

'What is the matter? You have something? Stefan must not catch it.'

As we sat down to dinner that day, Trudi announced, 'On Saturday I will go to my aunt. There are two women here — I make a mistake? — three women, one man and one child. This is no good.'

But for some reason Trudi could not travel to her aunt's on the day she planned, and when Arnie joked, schoolboy fashion, 'Your auntie does not want you. She says you must not come', she flew into a violent rage and broke a plate over Arnie's head. Like a true West Indian male who 'no cluck-cluck fowl-hen was going to knock', he gave her back thump for thump. Her nose began to bleed.

'You broken my nose. Call the police. Call them.'

'Oh Lord,' moaned Mattie. 'Arnie done dead! They going to kill him for knocking a white woman. Never mind the half-black baby.'

Stefan was also screaming like the siren on an ambulance. Trudi, with him in her arms, moved slyly towards the door, her face covered with blood. Mattie leapt up, her back to the door.

'You ain't going nowhere, lady. You going to have to use the windows. This man is your husband.'

'True, Trudi, you started it,' I said.

'*You* started it,' sobbed Trudi. 'He was a good man who turned bad when you came. You made him think in a primitive way — about his life of poverty. It is a trap for him —like a pig bathing in the mud. All of you love it.'

'Is true,' said Arnie. 'After all she is my wife. I must not forsake her. I know she is plain-talking. Always so damn plain-talking.'

He took Trudi upstairs, washed her face and made her tea. Then he went out to buy a piece of beef to prevent her having a black eye. It didn't. Mattie lent her dark glasses.

'She's got him doped. He's doped from his flies to his eyeballs,' said Mattie.

I sat there stunned by all that had happened.

When Trudi left two days later, Arnie was simmering with delight. He had a son, had reclaimed his wife's love and now he had the freedom of a bachelor. He lost no time in finding a new love — the betting shop, which he faithfully visited each day.

Pa wrote. The twins were getting married and wanted Mattie for their bridesmaid. Mattie explained that the men the twins had originally intended to marry already had wives, a fact they had neglected to mention. This time it was the real thing. We went to the Co-op in Camden Town and Mattie bought a beautiful, pale-blue organza dress. She was funny and entertaining and, with Trudi gone, we were free to talk, laugh and eat as we liked.

I sent Ma a pretty silk nightdress. I wanted her to pretend to be a rich woman, wrapped in luxury with soft silk touching her skin. She had taken no notice of her skin throughout her entire life. It was there, as far as she was concerned, for no purpose whatsoever, except, of course, to keep her poor.

After Mattie left, I decided that, come what may, I would get a job, but even as I sought work (and was frequently rebuffed), memories of her stayed with me, her presence like a spotlight on my every deed.

I went into a large store after seeing some black women cleaners at work and asked for employment. I spoke to a crisp, efficient, personnel manager.

'We have vacancies in the cold store.'

'I'll try any work.'

He gave me a form to fill out. At the end the manager said, 'I have to say that your handwriting and spelling are A1. Some that land up here are hardly literate. Stay here a few days and we'll see. What's your name?'

'Miss Hayley.'

'Not in the cold store, Sunshine. What's your name?'

'Em!'

'OK, Em. Report on Monday, nine o'clock.'

I smiled. I wasn't going to have him bawling Emelda at me! I threw the card at him and walked out. I went home simmering, but feeling quite pleased with myself. Still simmering a little, I waited for Arnie to come home. I waited till midnight. No Arnie. Two days passed. No Arnie.

On the third morning I heard a very powerful rap on the door. Whoever it was seemed in a tearing hurry. They rattled the door flap, rang the bell and pounded on the door.

I took my time. Then a raucous voice yelled, 'Arnie! You swindler! Are you in there?'

'No, he is not in here,' I called back, opening the door in some trepidation. 'What do you want?'

'Money,' a stocky man said, rubbing his fingers. 'He's been bettin' on account. He owes us sixty.'

'Sixty what?'

'Sixty pounds, missus.'

'Oh God, where will he get that money? It's over a month's wages.'

'I don't care, missus. Tell 'im I'm coming back Sat'day. If he don't 'ave the money, I will 'ave 'is guts for garters.'

I was ready to faint. Poor Arnie. I went up to his room. Behold! It was as empty as a pair of dead man's shoes. Arnie's clothes and etceteras were gone out of the furnished flat. A brief note said, 'I'll write. Tell Trudi the same.'

Sore and sad and eating humble-pie, I started my work in the cold store. I was cold when I went there and colder when I came home. It was dirty work. Horrible work. It sickened my stomach. And the man kept calling me Em and playing touch. A week was enough. I left.

After some thought, I applied for a job as a social worker. Because of my training as a teacher, I did not need much social work training except to learn about the laws and regulations concerning children and their rights. But there was much more to it than a bit of reading, note-taking and observation. Not only had I to stick to the law, I had to listen, share feelings with people and understand their position. I was interested in helping children and I began to feel exceptionally happy to be so involved.

My co-worker was a girl called Elizabeth — Lizza — a pleasant girl from Liverpool. She could pass as white but, if you

72

looked carefully, you could see that somebody was black among her ancestors. She liked the work, though she said she did not like people. We worked well together and enjoyed dealing with the problems brought to us. I felt useful again, but was still plagued by thoughts of Arnie. I visited his workplace. Like me they were ignorant of his whereabouts. I collected his wages and paid his rent for several weeks. Then I rented his room, without permission from the landlord, to a student from home.

Christmas came and went. Letters from Trudi began to pile up. I wrote back to her and to Pa to say that Arnie had disappeared. Her letters stopped. Had she heard from him? I couldn't tell. But I did receive a comforting reply from Pa. Ma, he said, was pleased that the twins were settled and had men to 'protect them'. She adored the nightdress I had sent. 'I won't wear it now,' she promised. 'I'll wear it when I'm going to Glory.' It was no use telling her that dead she would be unaware of the kiss of soft silk on her skin. Mattie had made a lovely bridesmaid but was plagued by asthma attacks because of the dust at her workplace. Jacko now sold used cars, worked hard and was being rewarded with success. Pa himself, deeply grieving over Arnie, hinted that he was planning to come over and comfort me.

I wrote back to Pa trying to reassure him that people did not just disappear, that Arnie was bound to show up. I paid the rent again and had a bit left over which I sent to Trudi. Arnie had done mean things to her but leaving her to fend for herself and the child was the meanest of all. But I also grieved for Arnie. Learning how to be a father to Stefan would have helped him fill in those missing pieces of emotions and feelings, lost in his own life through Pa's absence, bound as he was to long hours of backbreaking work on the plantation. We had both been deprived of a carefree childhood, but there had always been Arnie and me. Though we never played, we talked. Now he had vanished. The men of the yards had gone more deeply into Arnie than I thought.

I remembered hearing Ma say that as a child she had played hopscotch and rounders once or twice a year and had skipped now and then, but that her childhood had mostly been a troubled preparation for life. She and her sister had sat and thought and talked, but their talk was about how to survive and hold on to sanity.

I remembered, too, how when the women of the yards told stories, they were often full of hints and innuendoes about each other, especially when someone had behaved in a mischievous way, or needed consolation, warning or direction. These stories were fables, full of proverbs about how to deal with life, but they were also the means whereby the women acted out their personal feelings through tone of voice and gesture. I had to put my deepest concerns down on paper. I wrote to my family about my new work, and about the droves of men, women and children who were coming in from the West Indies to beat the new Immigration Act. I felt that no one was interested enough to understand what was really happening to these people and I had to express this in some way.

Like Pa, men came looking for work, unaware that their children needed care of a kind unknown at home. There were pressures on parents that enforced neglect of their children, and temptations that touched unsupervised children. Back home we were used to 'passing on' troublesome children to grandparents, but with nowhere else to turn, local authority children's homes became the 'grandparents' house'. The differences between 'home' and 'a home' were lost on some parents. Back home we had learned to regard Europeans with a mixture of fear and respect. The possibility of their unconcern and criminality was hardly considered. The 'homes' set parents free to work, in the same way as Mama Tat, Auntie Bet, Miss Daisie and Miss Lucretia set Ma free when they minded us. But we were never in danger of attack from people who hated our colour.

The twins sent me photographs of their wedding, and Mattie sent those she had taken of Arnie and me. Mattie was a little better, but her chest always gave her trouble in the cold weather. Troy had come back into her life and worked so that he could help her with medical bills. Jacko wanted her to go back home to live in the warmth and look after Auntie Bet's house, now Ma's and Pa's, but Mattie said that she, and not Jacko, would decide whether and when to return.

Lizza, my co-worker, was off sick and I was working on my own when a headteacher asked me to visit on an urgent matter which concerned a six-year-old pupil, Boscoe Shatner. He was evidently in distress but would not answer any questions. His mother had told him not to. I decided to try.

'Where is your mother now?'

'Gone to Birmingham.'

'When?'

He came close to my ear and whispered, 'Friday night with Dave. Don't tell them. They're not nice people.'

'Who gave you food?'

'Mum asked the lady next door to feed me and then I went home to watch TV and sleep. Mum gave her money. It was OK.'

'What, on your own?'

'Yes, I always stay alone when Mum's on the...' he stopped abruptly.

'What does your mum do for her work?'

'I ain't telling.'

'Do you know when she's coming back?'

He shook his head.

After a great deal of discussion, I decided to find a good foster placement for him, though he was such an independent, abusive little boy, uncaring and disrespectful of adults, that I knew this would be difficult. I asked permission to use the school telephone to began my enquiries. There were no foster places available. I had no option but to take him to a local authority children's home. When I told him this he started to cry and begged me not to put him in a home.

'My mum was in one. Please, please don't put me there.'

His tears came in a wash and his screams pushed his anguish into my heart, but it was my duty to send him to a place of safety. When I left him in the matron's charge, he was in absolute despair. He sat on the floor rocking and screaming, his agony clear for all to see.

The matron nonchalantly dismissed it.

'I've seen this before. They soon settle down.'

I rose to leave.

'Please, Auntie! Please! Please! They were cruel to Mum! They burnt her with a spoon. I hate them! Please don't leave me!'

I could hardly tear myself away.

The next day I visited him at school. He looked ill and would not speak at all. I waited to see if his mother would appear, as I had left a message for her. At about four o'clock, a small, stylish woman dressed in black leather from head to toe appeared. Her skirt was only just below the point of discretion. Her boots were thigh high, her jacket well cut and her hat distinctive.

'What's wrong with Busky? I made arrangements for him. How dare you put him in a home! I don't want you messing in my life.'

'You, my girl, are in trouble. You left this child alone for three nights. Suppose there was a fire!'

'Oh, rubbish! Where! I'm taking him home.'

'He's in care. If you visit the office, we'll tell you what you can do if you want to get him back. He will stay in the home and you can have weekly access. We'll inform you of the time of the case conference and hear your views then.'

She stood for a while chewing her gum, then she hugged her child and they cried bitterly. That was when I decided to become a foster parent. With the money left over from the legacy Mrs Penn had bequeathed me, I decided to set my sights on getting a house. One on a short lease would match my pocket. I wondered about starting at my present place, but decided against it because I still expected Arnie to return. Instead Pa came to see me.

I believed in the eternal spirit when I saw Pa. He had changed a great deal, but yet there was part of him still as I had always known him. Hard work, and harder times had left intact his spirit for us, his children, to sense and see. Only his legs had been slightly bowed by the years. Tears formed a thin curtain over his eyes, tears that had been hidden away for generations, in crevices he did not know were there — the tears of his ancestors and of his brethren. On his head he wore a jaunty, chequered hat and a matching jacket, as if to illustrate his chequered life. But he seemed more certain of his direction with the passing years. For the first time he wore a wristwatch to measure time. All his life Pa had recorded time by employment or lack of it, and by notching the names of those who had died and were returned to the earth. Time was the weeks spent in monotony, anxiety and deprivation.

Pa resisted the desire to hug me, for in his world to hug a lady in public was disrespectful, and not for men of his age. Men of his age still kept to what their slave forebears had learned, that affection had to be concealed with darkness. He put his hand on my arm as if restraining something in both of us, though even through the fabric of my coat I could feel the warmth of his greeting. We stood face to face for moments, before laughing and stifling the little emotional sounds that tried to break through.

'Melda,' he said at last. 'I prayed to see this day.'

Just as Arnie had led me to the taxis, so I led Pa and took the long drive home. All through the streets I relived my own journey, fitfully hoping that Trudi would materialise and stand by the door, her hair stringy and blonde, the false, pink spots of rouge on her cheeks like counterfeit coins, and her tongue awaiting opportunity to defend her ground. Wishful thinking indeed! No Trudi. No Stefan. No Arnie. Pa occupied, for privacy's sake, the room upstairs and was pleased with it, but for me, even going upstairs brought back Trudi's persistent talk, Stefan's cries and Arnie's protestations.

'I have two beds,' Pa said.

'So you can pick and choose,' I replied. 'It's a bunk-bed.'

We sat down to the meal I had prepared, but I relished more the God-sent company and long periods of loving silence between mouthfuls of good food.

'You, of all the children, Melda,' he said quietly, 'look like my mother. My father was from India, my mother black. His faith was Muhammedan, and he taught me that God, however shown, is always in your life and you must surrender to the will of God. I got blessings from both — my bones from my pa and my flesh from my ma. I see that flesh on you. God bless you.'

'Arnie just up and disappeared,' I said, ignoring the feeling of wholeness Pa was trying to convey. 'He planned to go because his clothes went too.'

Pa scratched his head, but I continued to tell on Arnie.

'He did not whisper a word. I thought he would "pinch" me and tell me. I thought we were close. Now he's vanished. All his clothes. He told Ma, the day Mrs Penn came to ask 'bout my exams, that I was wearing dirty clothes. He comforted me when Ma said I wasn't her child, that I didn't belong to her and that I was a child of pain.'

'Cruel words and far from truthful words,' Pa replied. 'You were the child of my love for a young girl — faced with sufferation and tribulation from the hands of a bruck-shirt, rough-tongue man. Her husband!'

'You sound like you rhyming calypso, Pa,' I giggled briefly. Pa expected girls to giggle to show they needed men to make them serious.

'No, is true! A long story but I will cut it short. My pa used to read out the story of a king,' he said. 'One day some hunters killed a bird and the king saw them and picked up the bird. The hunter-men surrounded him and wanted back the bird. "Cut off my flesh and take it, as much as the bird weighs," said the king. But as they cut, the bird grew bigger and heavier and they kept on cutting flesh till the king died. Well, before that happened, I said, "No! No more!" That was what her husband was doing — cutting away the flesh of her mind bit by bit, chunk and piece. She didn't know herself. She come to live with us — the opposite in every way to Ma. She was the only other woman I cast eyes on. She died when you born and I put you in my family.'

'What was she like?'

'Tallish and full-face like you, shapely and sly-laughing! Never gave offence. They called her sweet Mabelline or Sweety. She was a beautiful girl. When she was dying she said, "Don't cry, Henry. Sweety can see Heaven!" I gave her water and she died. For months my voice was trapped in my throat.'

'Ma did wicked. Ma used her brain, her hand, her head and her mouth to torment me, but she's changed and I forgive her. After all, she is my mother. I don't like that word motherless, so I claim her.'

'Hm. The Lord made each thing for its own end. He even made the wicked for the day of disaster.'

CHAPTER 6

I took some leave and Pa and I enjoyed the sights of London, for spring had come again and the daffodils were out, their yellow heads true and transparent in the sunshine. The clouds were higher up in the heavens than those at home, Pa said, and the people were not as many as in Harlem. 'And there you don't know for certain them that's begging for their bread when you land up beside them.'

The twins wrote a lovely letter to me, no matter it was poorly spelt.

'We are dreeming Jazz! And we're good! We'll be audishuning for the korus line in Jazz Train wich is going to London. If we get lucky we'll be thare. It is a musikal history of blues and jazz. We'll dance the Charleston for our peice. It is good to be marrid — to have your own guy to borrow from when you broke.'

Pa laughed heartily as I read on.

'I was certain they would never come to much,' he chortled. 'But there you are. They are two cussed beings but they are trying to keep straight. Taking the narrow path even if they tread on the life on it.' He smiled wryly at the thoughts he didn't express.

One morning, unexpectedly, Lizza's car pulled up outside.

'Hello, Melda! Crisis time! Come with me. I need your tact and your creole mind, holidays or no holidays.'

'What's up?'

'That Jamaican widower, that man whose wife died a few months ago. According to the school, he's been licking his three girls — especially the nine-year-old, who is a rude-girl.'

Leaving Pa to sleep, I set off with Lizza to see Mr Downer. Sadness had scarred his face and made him neglect himself. He had been pushed by circumstances beyond his powers to cope. He had not attended the case conferences, and one look at him and his house showed why. Chaos was close.

'What you two want now? You still minding my business? The headmistress been here, say I maltreating the girls. She say they have marks on their backs. And the council taking them. Is a big lie out of Satan mouth.'

'We'll take them until you sort yourself out. Then we will try and foster them, Mr Downer.'

I felt very sorry for them all and tried to reassure him.

'We will collect them from school and then come back and tell you where they are, and when you can see them, Mr Downer.'

'You must try and attend the case conference,' scolded Lizza in her schoolmarmish way.

'I working. If I absent I lose money for that! I not police like you two slaves.'

Mr Downer sat propping up his sorrows, one palm supporting his chin.

'Fourteen years of peace and bliss and God took her and left us. Why? We should have gone at the same time.'

Sobs racked his body.

'I don't want my girls put with an alien race, who had slave-master contact with black since time immemorial. O God! To think of it!'

He hurled himself on the floor, his face buried in the carpet, his neglected body working like bellows to send his breath steaming into the air.

Even Lizza, hard as nails, who thought him a 'snaky bastard' like her own father, who had run off leaving her mother to cope, looked away, her double chin quivering with emotion like a leaf in the wind. I made him tea, sat him in the armchair and, thinking of myself and my lonely tears in the dark, I wiped his face.

We left, too overcome to speak, and wrote our notes in the car. We pretended that sorrow, care and anguish soared bird-like, high above our heads. I had felt like telling him that I knew despair quite well.

When I returned, I told Pa about Mr Downer. He had reminded me of Ma's distress in my youth, but Pa missed the point and said, 'That could be a good man for you — at your age.'

I was twenty-seven. He had not seen Mr Downer, who most certainly must have been lusty and demanding — and forty-four.

'I can deal with women, Pa. That's what I learned. To be tender to women. Men rely too much on strength and performance and....'

'It's that Mr Walker's fault,' Pa cut in, the menace in his voice tenderised by age.

'Walker was a nuisance with a half-dead wife. I have work. There will be work and me together for ever — till the bird of heaven comes to bear me away.'

Pa smiled wistfully. 'Nobody spitting pepper at you. If you chose work is the good Lord fix it.'

'You know, Pa, I don't understand what they think of me at work. They don't always bother to invite me when they discuss things, but when they are taking black children, they always ask me to go along and help.'

'Don't think on that,' Pa replied. 'Just do what you have to do.'

'You have your own logic, Pa, but let's change the subject. How's your pipe these days? Still flourishing?'

'No. Mattie's chest put paid to that. In winter she's really bad. Ma wants to go and live in the house Auntie Bet left us, so Mattie can breathe sunshine.'

'You should go before next winter.'

'That boy Troy used to come round, but their family is not West Indian. We like our own people.'

'She going back to school? Mattie say she was not too concerned with that boy from the Projects — at least, so she said.'

'She's got no head for study. Too inattentive, like a horsefly — always looking for fresh dung. Troy talked his way in.'

Same old Pa, I thought. Same patchwork of talk.

I walked over to the window. The spring day was blooming like a ripe fruit, and the grass had a yellowish glow from the sunshine.

'I'll be going back to work soon, Pa. Will you be able to manage?'

'I survive New York. I'll manage. New York never clotted my faith.'

My desk was piled with 'cases' when I returned to work. I didn't mind this because I needed to work overtime for extra pay, to bring me closer to my goal of buying a house and fostering children. Pa never complained of my long absences. He helped me all he could and began to really enjoy his stay in London.

It was different to being in New York — a place to find work among others of his kind. But Britain was history, geography, kings and queens and Rule Britannia learned at school. The street names reminded him of streets at home, and it was not unusual for him to cry out, 'Look! Piccadilly! Look! Trafalgar! You remember Battle of Trafalgar when Nelson lost his one-eye!'

It was heartening to come home to find the lights on in the house, the radio playing and the smell of good cooking perfuming the flat. Pa cooked whatever took his fancy and I was grateful. He cooked savoury, filling meals and I felt that someone cared about me as Auntie Bet and Mrs Penn had done. Pa even baked bread.

Life, however, was bubbling away at home in Jacko's New York. His secondhand car business had grown, and he now owned a car lot. Ma saw him frequently but she still grieved for Arnie. She wrote to Pa telling him that she feared Arnie was injured, dead, or mad in an asylum. She had heard of such cases, all of which began with a disappearance, which led to loss of memory and then to more catastrophes such as 'spiriting away'. Ma's worries were Pa's too, and we decided to go to the Church of God to ask the group to pray for Arnie's reappearance.

It was a lively service. People were so bound up with troubles and suffering that their emotions could have served as banjo strings. Some of the parents were distressed that the children they had struggled to bring over had turned on them, resented them, plundered them and would readily harm them. They in turn felt guilty for neglecting or leaving their children. When they opened themselves to the experience of God, they celebrated his presence through singing and dancing. I too joined in when the Spirit took me over. Pa did not dance, but he testified to God's goodness when, as an outsider, he had gone seeking crusts for his family in a foreign land. Through that Church I came to think of myself as having been put on earth for a purpose and the light of life would lead me to it. Pa believed that too.

Young and old showed their respect to Pa and he was genuinely happy. He was leaving for home the next week, and the prayers and good wishes of the congregation went with him. I had known him as my father, feared and respected by all his kin. It never before occurred to me to seek out his gentler qualities. I simply accepted them as rare flashes of fatherhood when they surfaced. Now I knew him as a good man. I had observed his unselfishness, his humour, his capacity to mull things over and quarry thoughts about them from far down inside him, and then to act with decision. Pa had even taken a little job working in the market. He gave me three pounds a week to help me save. He was good to me.

After Arnie had vanished, my feelings of being protected had vanished too. Nothing bloomed inside me, only withered places remained. Pa had made them bloom again, and now we were parting, perhaps for the last time. But I had to put aside my own feelings; he was going back to Ma and Mattie who needed him, and whom he also needed.

'How old are you, Pa?' I asked on the train which took us to the boat.

'Fifty-nine.'

'And Ma?'

'Fifty-one.'

'You ever wanted to leave us? To go away from us?'

'To be honest, yes, only I never had the courage. It takes courage to walk away and leave your blood.'

There had been moments when his past suffering showed and he looked older, worn-out — used-up like a candle. I told him now how young he looked.

He laughed. 'The more man climb age, the more bones show. I shave every day, and the mirror shows me the real thing. I hope I see my three-score and ten.'

He took the boat at Liverpool to set off back to Ma, who I was sure would never visit me. She disliked travel and would journey only if she knew that waiting for her at her destination was either Pa or Auntie Bet or both. The bonds of blood and friendship united them and on that sea there was no dross.

I remembered an old rhyme:

What is a father but half of the heart
The other is mother, who gave me a start.

Pa, though, was both to me. Some colleagues talked of their

fathers as confused and prurient men, but my pa knew right from wrong at every hour of the day or night. He never trespassed over borders of intimacy. He knew that God saw and God knew whatever was done.

Just after Pa had left, the man from the betting shop came round again, for the third time, threatening to break my windows if Arnie didn't pay up. All these months and he hadn't given up yet.

'I don't know where he is. That's the truth! Arnie's not here. I can't help you.'

For weeks I could not sleep for fear of being burnt-out or attacked and hurt. I was so drained and worried that I thought about writing to Trudi at her aunt's, telling her of my predicament. But then I reflected that this was a family matter. What did Trudi care about us? I broke into my precious savings to pay off Arnie's debt.

I continued to find fulfilment in my work, in trying to help those immigrant families who were experiencing severe problems of adjustment. It was not just the hostility they faced. Some of their problems arose because they did not accept change and behaved as if they were still back home. With different conceptions of care, there were some who left their children alone for long hours, in rooms heated by paraffin burners, which were at risk of blazing up. Others, because they had lived in individual houses with their own doors, could not understand their responsibilities to the next-door or upstairs flat-dweller. And there were those who were evicted by landlords when they objected to the extortionate rents they were charged. The children were always the ones who suffered most in such situations and often had to be taken into care. Immigrant workers went from having a firm identity — of family, village, island or religion — to having only a nominal one: foreigner.

Lizza, a watered-down black woman, had no sympathy for immigrant workers and, sensing it, they would have none of her, and sometimes none of me either. But whereas I understood their anger, and carried on with my work, Lizza criticised, remonstrated, and told them what she thought of them. Her bigotry almost matched that of members of the League of Empire Loyalists who paraded each weekend with their flags and shouts of 'Keep Britain White'.

Lizza loved being paid, but she resented her work among the poor. She had a grand opinion of herself. She wanted to get married, but had not 'found anyone yet'. She talked as if she were looking for shells in the sand, and she was distressed when her mother accused her of being 'on the bloody shelf' at twenty-five. (Actually she was twenty-eight.)

She encouraged me to go dancing at the Lyceum, mostly among white people. Women danced unashamedly with other women. So many men had died in the war. So many sweethearts lost. I chose to be a wallflower when a man approached Lizza, who looked stunning, and asked her to dance. The dress she wore emphasised her proportions and the poor little man's height almost melted into hers. They danced constantly and seemed to be getting on like a house on fire.

On our way home she said, 'Well, what do you think?'
'Of what?'
'Of that boy. Carl Nelson. The boy I trod a measure with?'
'I don't know what you mean.'
'Shall I ask him to my place or shan't I?'
I shrugged. It would not have mattered what I said. She was like a hound with a scent and she was off.
'I'm not your mother,' I said. 'You want me to approve?'
In next to no time they were engaged and she invited me to tea. She was different in style, but very similar in intent to Trudi in her control of her lover. From the time we sat down she began drilling away at him. Occasionally she showed a

kind of gun-shot affection for him. After we had eaten he was under orders again. 'Do this for us, there's a good man. Do that for us, there's a good man.'

When he was out of the room she said, 'Well, what do you think? Should I or shouldn't I?'

'What do you mean?'

'Marry him. I suppose it would be OK. They settle once they bite the 'ook.' She giggled childishly. 'He's such a wimp. He's like water under my hug. There's nothing much of him. Some mother's "Charlie" most likely.'

'You're sure he's not moving towards the door?'

Raw terror rushed into her face. 'Not bloody likely.'

But in another month, Carl was off. His mother, he said, did not like Lizza, but said she could keep his expensive twenty quid ring. His mother said she wanted somebody younger for him, someone who was certain to be a virgin. Lizza was stunned but she did not cry. She smouldered and promised, 'Come Valentine's Day, I'll send that bugger chicken legs instead of a Valentine card. The turd!'

She kept her word.

As we continued to work together, she became more judgmental and disatisfied than ever.

'I am going back home,' she said suddenly. 'Mum said I might find something there. She'll help me.'

'I'll have to give you one cheer for persistence. The other two will have to wait till you succeed.'

'I'll treat the next one like eggs. Careful not to addle them,' she mused. 'We shall see.'

She left the following month.

I became an assistant rather than a trainee assistant after Lizza left and worked with Susan, a very well-brought-up, liberal, English girl. She believed that we were all born innocent, until the devil made us look another way. She believed everything she was told.

We had just returned a little girl to her mother, and Susan, insisting that they be left alone to get know each other, did not make any visits. Little Kayle was badly beaten for disobedience, and left alone while her mum went to an all-night party. The neighbours heard Kayle's cries and called the police.

I had the most awful argument with Susan. It didn't help when she kept on saying, 'How was I to know she'd do that?'

'Yes, how was she to know?' said the deputy, taking her side. 'We don't only want to be seen collecting-up children.'

I couldn't take the constant refusal to accept responsibility and decided that now was the time to start my work as a foster mother. I resigned from my post, borrowed some money from Jacko and bought a house in the same area as I was living. I paid two thousand nine hundred pounds for it. The lease was to run for fifty years — time enough to do what I wanted to do. The family of the old woman who had lived there sold me the furniture too, for I could never have afforded to furnish four bedrooms and two sitting rooms. I only had a little bit left over from Mrs Penn's bequest and the savings I had made when I was working as a teacher back home. This I guarded like my life.

I registered as a foster mother and, after being investigated and approved, I was allowed a small grant to buy other necessities. The first child who came to me was Boscoe Shatner.

When I saw him, I could not believe my eyes. He'd hardly grown. His face was pinched and sad, and the spunky light in his eyes had been snuffed out. His eyes were set like concrete and as he moved I was certain that a horrendous great animal was biding its time inside him. He turned to me with healthy distrust and snapped, 'Where are you taking me this time, missus?'

'Did your mum come visit you last Sunday?' I asked, trying to turn his doubts away from the present.

'I hate her. She's gone and left me. She never visits. She's gone with that David. He weren't my father. Just her ponce. The police wanted David and they've hopped it.'

'I'm taking you to my place,' I said. 'Come and try it. See if you'd like me to foster you.'

'And when I'm naughty, what will you do? Throw me in the dump?'

'Keep you. All children are naughty sometimes. Try me.'

Warily he walked towards me, the anger in him tumultuous and violent, but for the moment restrained. There was no love, none of the special quality that marks childhood. I tried to hug him.

'Don't touch me! Don't! I hate your face.'

We walked to the bus stop and then made our way home. But he made his reluctance to follow me crystal clear.

Over tea we hardly spoke. He deliberately set out to annoy me by biting into every piece of bread in sight, and then saying, 'I hate your bread. It smells horrid and it's dirty. I like white things. I want to be white.'

He switched my newly rented TV on and off, no matter what I said. When at last I called bedtime, I was almost choked to death with frustration.

'Come, I'll take you to bed,' I managed.

'Get off,' he said. 'I'm not afraid of anything.'

He was afraid of the dark but tried to conceal it by bluffing.

'I always have the light on. They turn it off when I fall asleep. I never ask them.'

He didn't tell me that his fear of going to the lavatory at night brought his pillow into use as cover for his big jobs, although he never wet his bed.

I foresaw months of hard work with Boscoe, who clearly felt utterly betrayed. But he began to react to my patience and clearly stated directions, and my sense of humour and care. I knew we had turned the corner when he sat on my lap and said, 'Auntie, take me to bed and read me a story, please.' At that moment he became my son. He didn't know what he had given me: the opportunity to indulge my need to mother.

A cablegram arrived from New York and my heart dropped to the floor. I could see drops of blood in front of me, even when I closed my eyes.

'Oh God,' I whispered. 'Give me courage to face this moment.'

I sat down and with trembling hands opened the envelope. Certainly Ma or Pa had gone. Surely Jacko had been killed from envy, the twins caught out in some shameful act, Mattie choked to death by asthma. Arnie discovered dead in some dreadful place.

My face lit up as I read on. The twins were coming to London with the musical show *Jazz Train*. They had played to rave reviews in every large city in America. They would be in London for a few days and then on to Paris.

Boscoe was beside himself with joy and anticipation.

'Do you mean we're related to people who dance on stage? Are you going to take me to see them? Wow, I want to go to New York.'

We prepared our humble, happy home to receive the twins. They would spend one night with us. Boscoe dusted tables and smoothed the beds a dozen times. He polished the banisters and swept the stairs.

At exactly two o'clock, a taxi brought the twins and they swept into the hall. On cue they peered into our sitting room, sniffing audibly to 'smell the place', as Ma used to do.

'Ah,' I said, 'here come the knives.'

But they smiled at me and said, 'You have a home, Melda. We have suitcases and hotel rooms, and we're the oldest. God bless you. You "been through" with Ma and we never pretect you.' All their years in New York had not taught them how to say "protect".

Boscoe ran in and, before being introduced, burst out with, 'Hello, Aunties! You are really beautiful! Please, Aunties, come to school with me tomorrow.'

I had never seen a child so excited before. He asked

questions about the show, and they told him about the history of blues and jazz, with poverty at the centre of the telling.

Next morning my chic twin sisters accompanied him to school. They did indeed look like film stars, and had the pleasure of hearing the teachers say what a well-mannered boy Boscoe had become, and what good things would come to him.

Just at this time I began to dream of Arnie. I was certain he was on some boat working in Africa or Martinique. I went upstairs, fell on my knees and thanked the Lord.

When we visited the show, it was my first visit to a real theatre. I was used to folk theatre at home, and great fun the plays were too. People joined in the dialogue and offered words and gestures that would better serve the ends of the stories. But that night, under the bright lights, among dressed-up, attentive English people, keen to enjoy themselves, my stomach turned to water. All I could recall was the folk theatre I knew—'Ruth and Naomi', 'David and Goliath' and 'Barabbas the Thief'. I closed my eyes and there were the twins rolling around on the grass! And there was me, the outsider, watching from behind the palms.

'O God,' I said, 'thank you for past and present.'

But as the lights dimmed, a new feeling arrived. I had become a child again, entangled in the wild vine of fantasy. Though Boscoe held my hand, I felt lonely. I had no right to be there. There were my sisters dancing with skill and delicacy on the stage, the footlights underlining the magic of their feet. When the twins changed from tap dancing to the Charleston, the applause was deafening, but none of it belonged to me. I felt jealous. I wished we could have changed places just that one time.

As the years had passed, they had become more alike, more together and less critical of the rest of us. The worlds in their heads still collided with those of others, but as a pair they were always in perfect harmony.

After the show, we went backstage to congratulate them and say our final goodbyes. I promised that when Boscoe finished his schooling I would send him for a holiday in New York.

I eagerly fostered children who had been caught up in short term family crises, and for longer periods those children who had been rejected by their parents. One day I was brought a baby of six months. The mother, a schoolgirl, had given birth to this child, perfect in every way except that, as far as the family was concerned, the father was black, a young man from Mauritius.

The social worker shook her head and said, 'Her father won't have the wee black thing in the house. It's like it was Beelzebub himself. The girl's mother said that touching it was like touching a monkey. I'm sure they'd kill it, given half a chance. They heap all their guilt and sin on this poor black bairn. No wonder the mother went looking for comfort. The man was very black — she could not possibly have loved him. Just a bit of him!'

I cradled the squirming little lamb in my arms. 'I'll foster him until you find someone to adopt him, though I'm sure his father's family would be glad to have him. Such children belong to their fathers.'

As it happened, two months later the social worker informed me that he was to be adopted by a white couple. He had been given a good biblical name by the nurses who looked after him after the mother was discharged. She hadn't given him a name, so the black nurses called him Gideon, because a whole band of them would be coming!

Boscoe surveyed him from a distance. 'I'm glad he won't be staying with us. This is a house for black people. Only his hair is black.'

'Out there is a world for all sorts of people,' I responded firmly. 'And they learn to live together in houses, churches, schools and other places. Colour should never be the first thing to consider. Character is what matters. Character is so much more important than colour.' I really believed that, though I knew it wasn't always how I felt.

He smiled. 'Sorry, Auntie,' he said. 'I never thought.'

Over the years, children came and went, but Boscoe stayed. Then one day I noticed a man looking at my house from across the road. I went out and faced him. He came right out and said that Dilly Karadee wanted to see her son, Boscoe.

'How did she find us?' I demanded.

'She didn't; I did. I'm a detective — a private eye. She's done well for herself. She's a singer, famous in France. Now she can afford to have her son.'

I managed to reply. 'Tell her to come tomorrow afternoon at four o'clock. The social worker must come too. I'll contact her urgently.'

The following day, Dilly arrived, dressed to the nines. Chic and fashionable, she behaved like a star, with expensive clothes and reeking of enough scent to set off a sneezing explosion in a convent. She had arrived with her companion, not David, the pimp, who had lured her away from her then eight-year-old son, but a smartly dressed, primly moustached spiv. Her son ran his eyes over her.

'You ain't my mum. She killed herself when I went in a home. She loved me. Now you've come, what do you want?'

'Don't be stupid, Busky. Your mama wants you. I'll go to court for you. I'm lonely for you. I want you. You're mine! And I didn't kill myself, as you can see.'

'I don't know you. You're not my mum. You look a bit like her, but you aren't her.'

'I know your secret,' she whispered in his ear.

'She knows! I did it here. I told her why. Because of David. Because I was afraid to get up.'

She wept while Boscoe remained calm. 'I'll stay with Auntie until I'm twenty-one,' he said. 'You said you would kill yourself if they took me. They did take me. So you are dead.'

'You ungrateful brat. You prefer this backward woman to your mother? This child-thief!'

'I'm not going with you, I don't want to. I'll stay here where I'm happy.'

'Well, you heard,' the social worker said. 'Plain as a bell he told you. We'll propose that he's made a ward of court and he can continue his placement in peace.'

Dilly sat motionless as Boscoe offered the guests cups of tea and then went out to play. He had his life and was totally unconcerned with hers.

She looked at me and said, 'I'm grateful for what you did. I had him when I was fifteen. He was like the black dolls they have in France. Unreal. Something to play with. I wanted my life. And fun. I get both in France. But there was never a day I didn't remember him. His face was a beacon for me in my struggle. And now! He hates me.'

What could I say? I had fostered him. I finally asked, 'Why didn't you write?'

'Nobody writes to children. And David was a wanted man. I was free when they got him. I'll do anything to get Busky.'

'Well, write to me. I'll send you a photo every birthday and his school report. He did love you once. Maybe it will come again.'

I watched her leave and climb into the little car her escort drove. Boscoe gleefully played cricket with his friends.

He came in later and refused to talk about her.

Apart from such threats to our household, my work continued to lift me to the skies, to bring me such fulfilment that I looked forward to every day. At night, though, I began to dream of Arnie again. He had always wanted to go to Africa and in my dream he was talking of Africa. He wore wings. I was certain he was dead. It would only be a matter of time before his bones were found. But I thought that if I acted

95

hastily and reported him as missing to the police, and then Arnie turned up, I might get in trouble or at least look foolish for crying wolf. Besides, Arnie was a man free to come and go. I gave Arnie up to God.

But, still plagued by my thoughts, I remembered our yard, adjoining Mama Tat's. I recalled all the women, those who wailed at the drop of a hat, and others who showed deep emotion just by gestures and tone of voice. I felt strange, so far away from them, their songs, their generosities — and their thoughtless dependencies. I wondered why Mama Tat, full to the brim of rolling rumbustious fat, was so called; and why Daisie, who was so far from that flower, had yet been named for it. I recalled how they sought approval from their men by giving them the best to eat and drink, how they ironed their shirts with a kind of smoking devotion, yet talked of them in the most reproving terms. It had its contradictions, but the yard passed on to all its peoples traditions that had been bred from the necessity to survive and to resist. It was the source of our dignity. It contained all that made us decent, self-respecting and black. Sometimes there was space in it for love.

The yard was the women's place, where the ghosts of dead women visited and lingered and enjoyed the fighting, the fun and the talk of children. For some, the one telling experience of their lives was childbirth — when they left childhood behind for ever and became women and mothers.

'God bless the yards,' I said softly.

SECTION FOUR

The lotus weeps to silver streams;
The river murmurs to the sea.
Red buds conceal the hungry worm;
Spent roses frown their tales to time.
Where is your heart, my worldly fawn?
Your flaming kiss consumes
The darkening moon.
Deep swaying shadows,
Flirtatious stars,
Tell me that love will return tonight.

CHAPTER 7

Ma, Pa and Mattie had returned to Guyana and were now living in Auntie Bet's old house, ours having been sold when Ma left to join Pa in America. In New York, Jacko had married Mary-May Devlin, an island girl. Mattie and myself were the only two, as Pa put it, without anchors. The twins were still performing in the clubs, although their dancing days were almost done. Still no word of Arnie. The odd Christmas card came from Trudi who had evidently returned to Switzerland.

I had now spent nearly twelve years in Britain. Thanks to Mrs Penn, I'd had a foundation to help my stay. Every bad winter, every ice-cold spring or so-so summer, I had vowed, 'This is the last', but here I was still in London, not yet able to understand the country. I accepted my given synonyms: foreigner, immigrant, dark stranger. As long as I lived here, that was what I would be.

I continued mostly short-term fostering during all those years, so that Boscoe could pay full attention to his school-work. He was gaining excellent marks and was a monitor. I kept my word to his mother, and she sent money to us from time to time.

Often I wished Boscoe would agree to see her, but nothing could persuade him. The scars of his early life turned easily to weeping sores, and he mused, 'She can't even protect herself. She loved being beaten up by her men. I used to see her.'

'She is your mother,' I would say. 'You should never talk against her. Protect her. You're her flesh and blood.'

'I want you to know, if it hadn't been for you — well, I'd be like a dog on the road.'

We talked, sometimes for hours, about my family and my life in Guyana, which, having been born in London, he found it hard to imagine.

A letter arrived from Pa saying that Ma was poorly and she might not be long for this world.

'I dreamed her end and she talks of it,' Pa wrote. 'Her bones are turning to water. I'm trying to steel myself — wondering what I will do after she is gone. I worked for her all my life, and gave her food and children. I'm sorry I could not give her fun.'

The pain and regret in his letter stirred bitter memories — some that I'd forgotten since fostering Boscoe. I thought of going to see Ma, but she rallied and began to stir in the yard. The crisis receded and Pa wrote cheerful letters. The sunshine and warmth of Guyana helped Mattie as well. She began taking private lessons to help improve her education.

Boscoe was now almost fifteen and still keen on his schoolwork. Then the news came that Dilly was dead — stabbed in a jealous rage by her manager and lover. Boscoe was beside himself.

'I killed her,' he wept. 'I wished her dead.'

He would not eat and woke screaming from his nightmares. What was I to do? Talk did no good.

I began to be affected too. My own buried wounds began to weep. Boscoe's social worker, who had lost her mother to German bombs as a twelve-year-old, visited us. She said that Boscoe needed to mourn for his mother; that he was blocked by guilt and grief. I remembered Ma and prayed for Boscoe.

One day I knew what we must do, and I picked up my boy and took him to France to see his mother's place, and know her times and things. We crossed the Channel without too much trouble, though the boat scared me. I felt it would roll over onto its side. The waves seemed so high as they rushed on endlessly towards us, I could only put my trust in God's protection.

When we disembarked at Calais, we took the train to Paris and then a taxi to the address we had been given. The people were 'singing their talk', even more than we did back home, but they were helpful when we told them through signs and gestures that Boscoe's mother had died and we had come to see her grave.

'Oh, comme c'est triste!' they said. 'Un garçon sans mère c'est comme la terre sans le soleil.' They were all moved by the fact that we had come to honour our dead. The taxi waited patiently to see if we had found the people who were meeting us. They took us to a modest hotel where we were to stay two nights.

It was a difficult experience to be in a strange country without the language, without knowing the customs of the people, but a group of Dilly's friends helped us find her grave. Later I took Boscoe to see the stage from which she had sung, and her dressing room and wardrobe where he saw the elaborate costumes she had worn. Boscoe stood among the costumes, surprise more than sorrow in his eyes.

'My mum was a film star — or like a film star. It smells good in here, but I wish she was here fussing her face like she did when I was little.'

Everyone, especially the cast of the company for which Dilly had worked, was sympathetic, courteous and helpful. The cast collected around five hundred francs, or fifty pounds, for Boscoe. Dilly had spent as she earned and left nothing much. They gave him her recording of her theme song, loved by the patrons. The words, printed on plain white card with a border of red roses, hung on one wall of her dressing room.

Le lotus se lamente aux ruisseaux d'argent;
La rivière murmure à la mer.

Les bourgeons rouges cachent le ver affamé;
Les roses passées désapprouvent leurs contes.
Où est ton coeur, mon faon mondain?
Ton baiser enflamme mord la lune assombrie.
Balancement profond des ombres
Étoiles flirteuses.
Dites moi que ce soir l'amour reviendra.

The lotus weeps to silver streams;
The river murmurs to the sea.
Red buds conceal the hungry worm;
Spent roses frown their tales to time.
Where is your heart, my worldly fawn?
Your flaming kiss consumes
The darkening moon.
Deep swaying shadows,
Flirtatious stars,
Tell me that love will return tonight.

'Play it for me,' Boscoe said and, when it was done, his pride shone like oil on his face as the sound of her voice filled the room. 'Again,' he begged. 'Once more.'

With a flourish, the director replaced the record on the deck and gave a repeat performance. The whole cast had assembled now and, in a moving tribute to the young performer, sang in accompaniment to her voice, its tunefulness filling the room like rare perfume.

Before returning home, we placed flowers on her grave. She was only thirty-one when she died. She'd had Boscoe when she was sixteen. He could now accept her death, for though to him she had died when he was eight, when being loved and wanted is a right and a necessity, he had never been able to grieve for her.

'Can we go now?' he asked. 'I know she's dead.'

He straightened up by the grave.

'Dilly,' he said sadly, 'I came to see you and I love you. I did that day, though I never enjoyed being with you. I hardly ever saw you. I'm sorry I ran away that time when David taught me a lesson.'

I squeezed his hand and we walked away. We went to a cafe and had some food. Boscoe did not eat much, but then he showed a sudden wish to explore the whole city — all in a day.

'Let's go and see the Eiffel Tower, the Mona Lisa and all the other French things,' he urged.

The visit was not planned for enjoyment, but we did enjoy ourselves. It was the first holiday I had ever taken in my life. People came to the Caribbean for holidays, but we went nowhere except to family parties, excursions and funerals for ours. Talk and song were holidays to us. We believed, as the old folk had done, that it was better to be bitten by your own bedbugs than those from the beds of others.

We returned home to a crisis. Social services were trying to place a young woman of seventeen who had been driven out of home and church for 'sinful conduct'. She was called Olive Greybrown.

'What could possibly cause your parents to shout "Sinner!" at you?' I asked.

'Nothing! I didn't do nothing. It's them.'

'Nobody will drive you away for nothing.'

'It's true, Auntie. I did nothing. The old men told me to! They are married to holy women — preaching, praying women. And they spend more time in the church than they spend laughing with their husbands.'

'So what's that to you?'

'They gave me money... to talk dirty and dance like Salome.'

I remembered that a film of that name was currently showing at the local fleapit.

'Where does all this dancing go on?'

'In the room where the men wait when the women are

laying out the food. One man gets me in a corner and says, "Dance, Salome, dance!" And I do. They give me money.'

'How much?'

'A ten shilling note. I don't take change. Sometimes I give a note to the collection plate.' She spoke as if the giving made the rude dancing acceptable.

I sat quietly, thinking about the size and taste of her brashness. I had Boscoe, an intelligent fifteen-year-old, to consider. What was I to do? I decided he should help me to decide whether to keep her for more than one night.

He questioned her and I listened. I heard her saying that he should try tackling the old men, and that everyone harassed young people as if everything was their fault. 'They should go after those old geeks who're so hung up on bad talk,' she concluded.

'You are old enough to know better. What makes you talk bad and dance dirty?' Boscoe asked.

'Because the men laugh. They glad to pay me. That was all I did. I danced and they made wicked things of it.'

'Well, put it behind you. Or you can't stay here. Don't let people make you act crazy. Have pride and self-respect.'

I was extremely pleased with my Boscoe; Olive would stay with us. I went to see her parents — rigid, uncompromising people. The father had started his own church. He hated sinners, and when his daughter turned out to be the devil's handmaiden, he hated her especially. Arms akimbo, dog-collar white as milk, he barked, 'I will have her back if she is penitent.'

'What do you mean, "penitent"?' I asked. 'How?'

'Take her punishment without complaint. She must be whipped.'

When I told Olive of this condition, she yelled, 'That cruel devil's not going to beat me. Nobody will beat me again, ever. My father got a kick out of beating us. He did it for anything, even if we ate noisily. He was always saying, "The eyes of God are always upon our deeds!" I try to respect him and I do, but...'

That was enough. She stayed with us until she'd qualified as a nurse and put her teenage performance far behind her. I was proud of her when she eventually qualified, just as I was proud of Boscoe when he came home one afternoon and told me he had come top of his class.

After my congratulations, he said to me quite suddenly, 'I knew my mum but I only saw my dad once, when he came to the home to see me. They know where he is, the social workers. Can we ask them?'

Then he added a question that must have been simmering in his mind. 'What will happen to the man who killed Dilly?'

'It was a crime of passion,' I said. 'So he will go to jail for life. He will not die.'

'I think that as he killed, he should die,' Boscoe replied without emotion.

At the next meeting with Social Services I asked about Boscoe's father.

'He is a Barbadian man,' the senior said. 'Much older than Dilly. He had a greengrocer's stall in Brixton market and she worked for him after leaving school. He's married. I think he has a family and his wife is English. I don't think she knows about Boscoe.'

My heart quickened. Lord! I thought, not another Trudi.

Unbeknown to Boscoe, I went one day in summer to the address. The door was opened by a woman who I assumed was Boscoe's father's wife. Passing as a relative of her husband's parents, I asked after him. She invited me into her home, offered me coffee and chatted amicably with me.

'He's not at the stall. We have a shop as well. He's there today. I'll draw a map for you.'

Thanking her, I caught the No 36 to the shop in Kennington. The owner was the most handsome and confident man I'd ever seen.

'I see where Boscoe got his looks from,' I said. 'Are you his father?'

'You know Boscoe?'

'Yes. Dilly is dead, stabbed in France and Boscoe is fostering with me. So I think we must talk.'

He looked around nervously. 'My wife doesn't understand our ways. She does not know about him. I never told her about Dilly. I read about the stabbing. I tried to find Dilly's mother but she had gone to the USA. I believe she went there years ago.'

'Boscoe said you visited him once.'

'I feel responsible, but I can't do anything about him. It's not only telling my wife. It's telling my two boys, both of whom are older than Boscoe. I strayed at a bad time.'

'You ashamed of him? He's a fine boy!'

'No! Never. He seemed a good boy. I'm ashamed at the way I treated his mother.' I left feeling sad. Up to the time Boscoe was fifteen years old, his father had not bothered about him. Boscoe had never had the chance to get to know his father although the same blood flowed in their veins.

Mrs Greybrown relented and came to visit her daughter.

'Olive,' she said in friendly greeting. 'You so bitter and bad. You're killing your father!'

'How can I? I haven't seen him for so long!'

'We never cease praying for you.'

'I never felt anything. You should have prayed for those wankers who hated being old. And Dad. What do you think he does to the virgin flock? The old women are stale! The old men want fresh young girls to shake their tits at them!'

'Don't blaspheme! Blasphemy is mortal sin!'

'Call truth mortal sin if you like. To tell you the truth, I was oft in danger, oft in woe, while Dad bawled, "Onward Christians! Onward go!"'

'Stop, Olive! Don't show off! You're talking to your mother!'

'Mrs Greybrown, this is not helping you nor Olive. Come back in better weather. Give Olive a few more years to thaw out.'

Mrs Greybrown tossed her head and said, 'She is dead to her father. Now I say, to me too! Me too!' I watched her waddle away — self-righteous and unforgiving. Where was God in all this? But I was very angry with Olive.

'Never,' I said, 'never talk like that in my presence again.' She pouted and then burst into a storm of tears.

Around this time, Trudi sent me a handsome photo of Stefan, now growing fast. There was no word of Arnie and I wondered if she had divorced him. I was certain that she would not have gone short of anything. Her life would include low-spots where she would whine and complain, but there would also be merriment, pamperings and indulgences. Her needs were greater than everybody else's, and she could whine the fleas off a dog. She never wrote of Arnie and I felt angry that he mattered so little to her. It was as if she had exorcised him from her heart, and erased the sound of his name from her thin-lipped, pink mouth that so sharply expressed her opinions.

I wrote her a letter deploring her attitude to Arnie. Back came the reply: 'Arnie was always in the house when he was with me. When you came, Arnie hated the house, and found fault with me. Maybe there is voodoo with you, and you used it on Arnie to make him not to want me or Stefan. If I knew where Arnie was, I would not tell you.'

This was typical of Trudi. The truth was I knew nothing of voodoo. I had been brought up on prayer, the Bible and the goodness of God, all my life. Now Trudi was Trudi and sometimes a little green lizard ran across the dusty path of her mind and hid itself in the tall grass and brittle rubbish that the war and the violent death of her parents had left there. Had Arnie told her that in the yards, half a mile from ours, women held Cumfa dances to honour the goddess of the sea and threw food and flowers on the water? How Arnie had chirped to that woman! But even wagging his tongue like a dog's tail, I prayed to see him again.

It was then that I began to think about going home to visit Ma. I could send Boscoe to Janine, a French friend of his mother's, who had invited him to spend some time in her family. Social Services had already offered to pay for a holiday for him. Before this time, my memories of Ma and my childhood were so bitter I had never once felt the desire to go home. But Ma's health was again up and down and everyone knew that one day her name would be called. I heard again her feeble singing of her favourite hymn:

'When the roll is called up yonder
I'll be there.'

I began thinking about what all those who had passed over were doing: Mrs Walker, Auntie Bet, Mama Tat and so many of Pa's friends who had been taken in unexpected and terrible ways. But our pa and ma were still with us. We had sung in praise of Pa's love for his children, but what of Ma? I had learnt something deep from Boscoe when we were in France.

CHAPTER 8

Bad news of Ma's health reached me again. It was now imperative I saw her. 'Her heart is slowly giving up the struggle,' Pa had written. The twins were already on their way home. Jacko, though, could not leave his pregnant wife, and Arnie, of course, was still missing.

I sent Boscoe off to Janine in France, placed Olive in charge of the house and wrote a strong letter to Trudi. 'Please, if you know where Arnie is, tell him that Ma is dying. He was her first-born son, her favourite. Surely you should wish Stefan to know when you are dying.'

She sent a cablegram: 'Do not know Arnie's whereabouts. Would not tell you if I knew.'

So that was that. How I despised that woman, who said she loved her husband and yet would deny a dying mother the sight of him.

I went back home and, reunited with Mattie and Flora and Florizel, railed against Trudi and all her race. Ma's breathing was giving her problems and Pa sat beside her, fanning her, and trying to set a breath-pace for her.

It darkened outside and we were certain Ma would die that night. We took turns to watch her, but in the morning she rallied, and drank a little coffee. She whispered, 'Where's Arnie? Where's my son? Arnie coming?'

'Yes, Ma,' I lied. 'He is. I got a message. He knows you won't go without him saying goodbye to you. He's coming all the way from Africa.'

'Good,' whispered Ma. 'Africa is a far walk. Today is the day. My bones melting. Turning to water. Arnie must come. Only my leg bones are hard. I have to drag myself into Heaven. I know Africa is the farrest place you can think up.'

I felt desperate. Ma was struggling for breath. Pa was musing, 'You bring up you children. You work in praise of them and then this; they absent at this time.'

'Oh, Pa, don't judge. If there's a God he'll make a miracle for Ma,' Mattie consoled.

Everybody was so burdened that we did not see anything or hear anything. The door opened and a figure appeared. The good Lord had made a miracle.

'Arnie!' I shouted. 'Where you been all these years?' I began to thump him and cry.

The twins screamed, 'Pa, Arnie come!'

Mattie sat in the chair puffed up like a bullfrog. 'Ma is dying because of you,' she said. 'You ungrateful hog. You bewitched! You sinner! You will be cast to the Devil.'

'Don't judge,' said Pa. 'Just thank the Lord!'

We crowded round Ma again. Only Jacko was missing. Pa brought in a glass of water.

'Each of you give Ma a teaspoon of water. Each of you in order of birth.'

Outside, the women sang songs and hymns so that Ma's soul would find the paths of Heaven and 'go quick and walk good'.

Crying and sobbing, each of us gave Ma water as Pa held her head up. He gave her water too. And then he said, 'She'll go in the late afternoon. Jacko is on his way. I feel it. Ma is waiting for him. God will forgive and bless him for making a choice to leave Mary-May and come.'

We kept watch on Ma's spirit till late afternoon and Jacko did come! He gave Ma her last drink; she could not swallow all of it. She died peacefully while the water ran out of her mouth. We cried bitterly for Ma's life that had known so little of peace, pleasures and plenitude. But there she lay, with pleasure now on her face. She had seen God.

There was nothing that had to be prepared. Everything had been made ready: Ma had set out the hymns to be sung and the prayers to be read. She wanted us to speak at her funeral, to talk of her kindness and her cruelty, her silence, her madness and the struggle with the mushroom. In her later life she had shown us all more affection. It did not come easily, but she could be kind in her offhand, restricted, dammed-up way. Now she would be kind in spirit.

The wake was held and Ma was buried at ten o'clock next morning. The village helped Pa to bear his grief. He sat in a hammock in the yard while different groups of people sang hymns to him, and prayed for Ma to be greeted by all the saints at the gates of heaven. Before we could give full care to Pa, Arnie had to explain himself.

'Where were you these eleven and a half years, Arnie? Nearly twelve whole years.'

'These last few years I've been in Switzerland, with Trudi and Stefan, and my daughter Jacqueline,' he replied tearfully. 'Before then I worked on a boat, then I went back to Trudi. She wanted to go back to Switzerland, and there we stayed.'

'And you never wrote to me, to Ma, to Pa?'

'Well, Trudi said you would come and get me. And we would fight again. I'm happy in Switzerland. I'm a man there. A husband, a father. I was able to start from scratch. Be somebody. Live like a man — not rich, not poor, just a man.'

'What about me, Arnie? I had to pay money for your gambling. I was frightened.'

'I didn't want to come back. I was happy. I did different things. I even went to school and learnt about electricity and plumbing. I have a trade now.'

'You were selfish,' said Flora. 'A true brother is never selfish.'

We couldn't accept Arnie's rejection of us. For us, whatever relationships we made outside the family, family still came first. Arnie had turned his back on our ways; he was part of a world which put a wife higher than a mother.

'I name my daughter after Ma,' he said by way of reconciliation.

'We will never see her. Ma didn't know. She couldn't tell the yard you name your girl-child for her.'

'Trudi is at the hotel with the children. She's afraid to come here uninvited,' he said.

We buried Ma's flowers that afternoon, after everyone had seen them, and talked about her for nine days. Pa was comforted by the hymns that were sung nightly, reassuring him of Ma's place among the angels.

Arnie often sat alone as if he was unable to face us heart to heart. He could explain only to Pa, who pretended to understand. I couldn't, but some cantankerous devil took me by the collar and dragged me to the hotel to meet face to face with Trudi. I did not smile. I wanted to shake her and yell, 'How dare you! You blonde monster!'

She sat in the lobby with Stefan, a handsome, edgy boy of twelve, and her pretty, self-assured little daughter, Jacqueline. I stood looking daggers at Trudi as she said, 'Stefan, Jacqueline! This is your Auntie Melda. You must shake her hand and hug her.'

The children obeyed her like two well-dressed robots.

'Why do you hate us?' enquired Stefan. 'You don't look very nice in your eyes.'

'Well, I haven't seen my brother for many years. If there's anyone to hate it is my brother — the delinquent.'

'Yes, but he is only your brother. He is my papa. And I must respect him.'

Trudi was concentrating on her needlepoint, with only a slight reddening indicating that she had heard or was interested in what her son had said. She was not, however, done with me.

111

'You better go,' she ordered, without lifting her eyes.

The children said 'Goodbye' together, and I left at once.

The very next day a woman visited us. But none of us had bargained for what we got. She looked so peculiar it was not too difficult to recognise her! It was that woman — no matter how she tried to pretend. Her hair was so unreal, it had to be a wig — black and tightly curled, and her skin darkened so she looked like a grotesque minstrel show. But she could do nothing about her eyes. They were as blue as summer skies and as penetrating as they had always been.

'Trudi,' I said, 'what are you doing? Playing games to laugh at us? You laughing at our sadness! You fooling yourself again!'

Mattie and Pa and some of the women of the yards had by now gathered. They eyed her up and down.

'What you doing, Trudi?' I yelled. 'You never going to stop insulting us? Fancy coming here masquerading as a God knows what!'

'If I come as Trudi, I am not welcome! Why? Because I am not black. Well, now I am black! Yet you do not accept this? What difference does it make to you? You are prejudiced! You have colour in your head like a disease! You are sick with hatred of those of us who are white. There are many different peoples in the world.'

A murmur of support for her point of view ran through the crowd.

'She' — jerking her head at me — 'hates what Arnie loves. She would not let me respect your mother.'

Another murmur, and this time accusing looks at me.

'Arnie is a judas,' I yelled.

'Why, because he hid from your malice? The hate-seeds that you tried to plant between us?' Trudi countered.

'Can't you see,' Jacko intervened. 'She thinks you wanted to break them up.'

Trudi nodded, as Arnie came in with the children.

'Please, Trudi, take off that stuff,' he pleaded. 'That wig! It's not right. You make yourself absurd to prove a point. You look ridiculous. Come in the house with us.'

'You must all ask me. Even Melda. She cause this,' Trudi said tearfully.

She was angry and Pa gently put his hand on her shoulder. 'Glad you come to mourn with us, Trudi,' he said. 'Now, bring your children in to us.'

'I lived through the war,' Trudi suddenly broke out, without moving. 'Many bombs. I met up with a poor man-student from the Gold Coast. I was thirteen years old. I was not afraid. I led him to safety through the woods. I did not notice he was black. I was thinking of my life. Your daughter never had to walk with death. I had never seen such a man before. Nobody had, but everyone had feelings for his life!'

I could not stay silent. 'What do you know about me, my life, my feelings, Trudi? What do you know?'

'Nothing, except that for you everything must be black or you hate it. You make music on the piano with black notes and white notes together.'

'Life is not a piano,' I replied scathingly.

She bit her lips to contain her anger. 'I did what I had to do and I'll do it again,' she said.

All I could say was, 'When are you going back home?'

'When Arnie has had enough. I'm sure he will not stay any longer to get... how do you say it? Tarnished.'

'Arnie grew up here. He's like us. *You* have the sharp edges that cut and cut.'

'In some things, yes, but being a husband, my husband and our children's father means that I must train him to be good at those jobs. I do not hate you but you try to make Arnie change back to being too much a man of this place. I want a man of my country.'

'Well, you should have looked there.'

'How do you know who you will fall in love with? You did not fall in love with anyone. You were too busy looking to whip my Arnie's legs.'

I said stiffly, 'Goodbye, Trudi. You have not changed.'

'Goodbye. Stefan and Jacqueline, say goodbye to your auntie. You must get to know your other aunties, and your uncle, and best of all your grandfather. Your Opa.'

'Yes, tomorrow,' said Mattie. 'See what tomorrow brings.'

Even with sorrow in my heart, I was still agitated and churned up. What had made Arnie reject us so completely? It could not only have been Trudi. What had we done as a family to make him feel trapped, to make him want his independence so fiercely? Arnie, even when present among us, was not with us. He did not want to be like us, in fact we had become his enemies.

Mattie shrugged at my questions, so did the twins. Understanding Arnie was beyond us all. He was a coward and had hidden inside his wife like a mole underground. Jacko agreed that Europeans always had to be in control. Pa kept his counsel. So we gave up trying to recapture Arnie, who came and went, and eventually presented his children to us as he should have done in the first place. They delighted Pa and chatted unself-consciously with everyone.

Eventually Trudi came back to our house and began to explain herself. 'I was afraid,' she said. 'Arnie talked constantly of you all and I was afraid to lose him. I had already lost all of those I loved. I did not want to lose Arnie and so would not share him. Do you see?'

We did see, but only in part. There was as yet no way in which I could embrace Trudi as my sister-in-law, and her children as niece and nephew. The twins felt the same, but Jacko and Pa continued to talk in praise of love and children, and pleaded with us to 'suffer the little children'.

Trudi could not understand what families like ours had been experiencing, when families like hers sat around the table eating meat, potatoes and dumplings. She owned Arnie, treated him as her mother had treated her father, and he delighted in it. Her behaviour was so outside his expectations that he wanted encore after encore, and his greed for Trudi's milk, whatever kind it was, made him forget us, his roots.

I decided to stay with Pa until everyone else had gone. One day I went to our old house to see what the people who had bought it had done to it. They had completely built over it and with its disappearance our childhood was gone for ever — leaving only memories that each of us would shape to serve our own ends. I gave the house one last look of goodbye. It had nothing to do with me any more. The corrugated-iron roof, glass windows and a doorbell that went pling-pling all had nothing to do with me. Our old home was gone and I could not point my finger at anything and say, 'This made the house our home, and this, and this.'

All I could think of as special were the trees behind the house that threw dark shadows at night, and the grass in front, a worn green blanket on which the twins had once rolled around.

It was not the only thing that made me feel that I did not belong anymore. Already the talk had started, with people describing me as surly, determined, hell-bent. For me there had been no greater hill to climb than Ma and her wicked ways, but she was dead, and dead people have always been good in the mouths of the living. I was more than ready to leave, to go back to see Boscoe and Olive.

SECTION FIVE

Home, the place of fire and foam!
Of slippery joys and thoughts
That roam,
Of pebbly walks and thorny paths
And moments fraught or tender.
Home for some a place of bliss and wit
For others — just dead bones and grit.

CHAPTER 9

Home was now Auntie Bet's house — a beautiful wooden house that smelt of furniture polish and disinfectant, but it still did not feel like ours. We had not fought each other there, tended Ma in her madness, carved out preferences, found our favourite corners. We could not oil the hinges of the doors, for we could not locate those that squeaked. The house was unknown to us, so newly given it was.

Our house had responded to the invasion of rain by the flurrying of its thatch and its courting of the sun. Here, at Auntie Bet's the rain came down in a fan, then it splintered and became a pool. Water ran into the gullies and the grasses shook and shivered a little. The drops of rain flowing rapidly down from the galvanise thudded on the ground. The thuds at the back of the house could clearly be heard. I did not care for the house. It had lost its countryness, that house with the iron roof. The wind blew cold and pushed itself into the room through the windows.

We were uncomfortable there. Arnie sat saying nothing. It was as if words would rot his teeth.

'I never liked this time of year,' I said. 'What would it be like in New York now, Pa?'

'The Fall colours would be good,' he said.

'Arnie,' I said, 'You should go to New York. Jacko needs help in his business. You are his brother.'

He thought for a while. 'If I tell Trudi —'

'She will say, "Don't go".' I burst out. 'She does not understand family. Soap, water, pots, pans and needlepoint mean more than family to Trudi.'

'I'm my own man, and I say no. Besides, I may not worship Trudi but I worship my children and they have their lives in Switzerland. When Pa went to New York, he left us behind. Many times I used to wish Pa was with us. I don't want my children to feel like that, to worry as I did.' He hesitated. 'Pa never hugged me once in my life, did you, Pa?'

Pa pinched his chin, as he always did when embarrassed.

Was this what we had failed to do that would have made the family bond with Arnie? From the day I met Trudi in London I sensed that something had been wrongly done. He had not involved me in his wedding, he had not wanted me to be part of his new life. He pretended indifference to Trudi but loved her dearly — her efficiency, her candour, her determination. He loved all these qualities.

'Would you like to see my house, Sis? I have some pictures!'

He showed them to me, photographs of a nice house with flower boxes on the window ledges, a suppressed glee on his face.

'Who planted the garden?'

'Trudi and me. We did everything.'

'Nice. You have a lot of white-people trimmings from Trudi.'

'She's a good homemaker. She sells her needlepoint for good money. I feel pride. I get respect.'

'Don't let it break your back or drive you mad,' I warned. He shrugged.

I tried to understand Arnie better after that, but did not always succeed. He did not want to be a part of our world. He saw us as always at the back of the class, overworked like Jacko — getting more embittered with the years. He did not see any of the good things of our life. Trudi had put new flavours in his mouth. I still couldn't help hoping they would make him vomit blood — the Judas Iscariot. He was going to the grasshoppers' ball riding on his mistress's frock, even if he had to turn flea to do it. What makes a man so blind? I could only conclude that Trudi had given him access to other realities and, whereas we thought him impoverished, he felt enriched.

He and his family returned home, and Pa promised to visit them. Whether he would or not was in the future, in God's hands. Jacko, who had left first, telegraphed that his wife had given him a daughter, whom he named Melda after me. The twins rushed back to their husbands. I made my preparations to leave. Only Mattie stayed with Pa. She, who had gone round and round the tamarind tree with Troy in New York, finally got together with Barrymore, who used to walk around with the rum bottle when they played 'drunk-man'. Now Barrymore had found a ready-made bed to sleep on, and a table to put his feet under. Mattie soon became quite the devoted little wife, and Barrymore was working as the village postman. His mother, (who christened herself Mrs Munroe-Patek, though there had never been a husband, even in a glass of fortune-teller's water), was not pleased, because she had wanted a 'girl of colour' for her son. He, though, a funny fellow over six foot tall, his body long and wiry, his legs skinny and bowed, seemed perfectly satisfied. Pa said he was too lazy, once he had sat down at home, to turn his head in any direction other than the one Mattie showed him.

When I got back to London, Olive and Boscoe met me at the airport and I found everything in order and happy. I rapidly took up my work again and life returned to its usual routines. But I felt a restlessness I had not experienced before. Olive was no longer being fostered by me and had become my lodger instead. She helped me with the children, but she was soon to finish her training and would probably be moving away to work in another hospital. Boscoe, too, would be leaving my care before long.

I was also feeling that perhaps I needed a break from the demanding work which I had been doing for so long. The children I was now getting were even more abused, trauma-tised and demanding than those I had cared for in the past. Perhaps I needed to recharge my batteries.

But I suspected that what my restlessness was really about was my family.

The children who came to me now were the victims of the worst kind of devilry: beatings, starvation, neglect, torture all were used against them to further the ends of those who 'cared' for them.

There were the three little girls who came. They were darlings, but they were extremely greedy. They would follow anyone to the ends of the earth for a crust. As soon as food appeared, their faces perked up like dog's ears. They were always ready to eat and were never content as long as there was more food to be had. I could not understand their preoccupa-tion with food until the social worker said, 'Oh, they had the most awful time. They have been so starved of love that they clutch for any comfort. The mother had a breakdown and they were farmed out to a woman who believed that food, mainly biscuits, cakes, sweets and chocolates, cured anxieties — crying, distress, everything. They are addicted, not hungry. It's an addiction showing up as greed.'

They would come home from school like little hamsters with hoards of food. Kindly dinner ladies had pitied them, 'Poor little mites', and were certain that I was neglecting them and not keeping up their constitution with suitable and sufficient food.

One day they were snatched from school and before the authorities could be alerted, spirited out of the country. I was later told that the father had colluded with a woman to pass as their mother. She led them out of the playground to a parked car and they were driven off. They sometimes came home for lunch, so no one had taken their disappearance as a matter for concern. I spent hours wondering what had happened to them and could only dread their fate at the hands of their father, who was suspected of abusing them.

I had learned from searing experience that I should not allow myself the privilege of attachment to the children. Their stay was a temporary arrangement, perhaps for a long time, perhaps for a short time, I could never guess. Distraught or not, when the time came for parting, it was a 'fait accompli'. Some returned to visit, others did not.

Fostering is like sunset and also like dawn. Its ingredients are complex: joy, pleasure, fellowship, but also ingratitude, suspicion and resentment. Even parents who do not want their children require and demand their love, and resent it being given to 'outsiders' whom they do not know and may not like. When confronted by people who resented me, I would recall the camaraderie of the yards, and the wisdom of Mama Tat —always the coryphee in the ballet of impoverished living.

Delmot, who now works as a painter and decorator, owes his life to Mama Tat. He came to me suicidal and unable to help soiling himself — particularly at school. The sole black boy there, he was daily surrounded and teased. There was no escape when the children got hold of him, shouting, bullying and laughing. He either hid after losing control of his bowels, or wandered off, foul-smelling and frightened. His condition was worse than any child I had ever met. He behaved like a cornered animal. I was on the verge of refusal, but Mama Tat's face flashed before me. 'Help him!' she seemed to say in her flat, matter-of-fact way. 'Surely you understand.' I did. We took him in. With hard work, he gradually learnt to trust us. I shall never forget his first real laugh. But episodes like this wearied me in a way they had not done before.

Then Pa wrote to say he was going on a visit to Arnie's place, as he put it — as if Arnie owned the whole country. Since Ma's death, we had arranged to share Pa. He would spend four months each with Jacko, Mattie and me.

Now we would each lose a month of Pa. Trudi wrote to reassure me that Pa would be fine with them. They were expecting him and all the family were excited at the prospect of his visit. So Pa went, joyfully, to mend fences with Arnie, his first-born son, who still occupied a special place in his heart.

I received a letter from him a few days after his arrival. It was a good letter and he told of the beauty of the mountains and the streams, the blessed greenness of the fields, the eloquent clouds and the poignant colours of both wild and cultivated flowers. 'I am happy that I have come to see Arnie's home and children brought up well and good, and carefully tended. Trudi cooks sweet-tasting food that invites you to eat because she is so stylish in the laying out of it. She makes me laugh. She talks like a drillmaster. It is still a slight sadness that Arnie chose white, but I like it here and will stay the full three months.'

I knew what he meant. Trudi was so white you felt different just looking at her.

Although the thought that I would lose a month with Pa still distressed me, I was so absorbed with children whose care needed all my energies and concentration, that gradually I put my upset over Pa out of my mind as I threw myself into crisis after crisis. But one Sunday night, I could not sleep for anxiety and turmoil and I could not understand why that was. I have always had strong nerves, but on that night my nerves were fraught. I fell into a fitful sleep and it did not deepen. I heard the rustle of papers in Boscoe's room and knew that he was reading. The little five-year-old in the cot in the room next to mine whimpered and called out, 'Give me my hat!' After that I fell asleep.

At about three o'clock I jumped out of a most frightening

dream. It was so real I took several minutes deciding what to do. Pa was getting all upset looking for his overcoat. Trudi was crying and hurling herself about as she did in the old days. Arnie tried to comfort her and I sat watching them as bewildered and confused as I used to be. I found the overcoat and put it around Pa's shoulders. Clear as a bell, I heard myself say, 'All right, Pa. You're going now.' I was furious with Trudi for upsetting him on account of the coat. It was all very real. I lay down again and woke up with my usual seven o'clock alarm.

We had only just sat down for breakfast when a cablegram was delivered to me. I never liked cablegrams. They threw me into a simmering state of dread. My stomach churns and all the terrors of Ma's mad times return. I sweat profusely and drink gallons of water. All my physical systems malfunction.

I began opening the envelope hesitantly and then, taking the bull by the horns, I tore it open and scanned the words.

I screamed. I screamed three times and hurled myself on the floor, beating the carpet and crying, 'Pa! Pa!'

The children of the house crowded round, as we had crowded round Ma.

'Auntie crying,' said a young voice.

'She's very crying,' someone else chipped in.

Boscoe came running.

'My pa is dead,' I said. 'I always had my pa. Even when he was slaving in New York.'

Boscoe telephoned Lizza, my friend from years before. We had kept in touch after she'd moved away, married and had a son. Her husband was a seaman. She agreed to come and stay as he was away at sea, so I could go to Switzerland.

That settled, my heart a lead weight, I continued my work, comforting the children, telling them little stories of my pa who was dead and whom I would never see again. They comforted me with their artless remarks. I still could not believe it. Pa was only seventy and his health had never given us cause for concern. He, though, had always joked, telling me, 'My strength is going somewhere. I couldn't tell anybody where it's going. Sometimes I think it's almost gone.'

Early next morning, Jacko arrived from New York on his way to Switzerland, to discuss how we could take Pa back home. Jacko thought we should cremate Pa there and bury his ashes with Ma. I began to cry.

'You going to burn Pa? How can you burn Pa?'

'Sis, is the best. It will be too expensive to take him home, too much money. Pa is dead. He will not feel.'

The idea of cremation distressed me. It was wrong for Pa. Pa walked slow, ate slow, did everything slow. Why should fire greedily finish my pa?'

All the time I was packing, my thoughts were rolling round and round. I took hold of myself and reined myself in. The children, I had to think of the children. Their lives must not be disrupted. When Lizza came, I was happier. She had mellowed, and her little son, Zimri, was a beautiful, plump, biscuit-coloured boy. She had gone back to her roots.

So we went, Jacko and I, to cremate our pa.

It seemed as if the flight was two months, instead of two hours, but we finally arrived and checked in at our hotel. Arnie came over and took us to see Pa. He was lying peacefully, dressed in his suit and tie.

'He had a heart attack,' Arnie said, bewildered. 'It was so quiet. Not a word to anyone. He drank his own glass of water. The glass toppled over with his last breath.'

He sat down, limp as a leaf, unbelieving. I thought he would never go home from the chapel and leave us with Pa.

Jacko, always silent or short-in-words, cast his eye over Arnie, the outsider — the black man with the ivory heart.

'We don't want strangers, Arnie,' said Jacko. 'This is no picture show. Just family.'

Arnie shook his head and went home. We remained with Pa for a while, with me talking to him and explaining my love for him, with my hand on his cold, rubbery, greyish brow, and with poor Jacko crying and regretting that he hadn't done more for Pa.

Poor Pa lay dead among strangers. At two o'clock we returned for the cremation. Surprise nearly killed us! The little chapel was crowded with white people, like creatures from another world, who had seen Pa walking by the river, who respected Arnie and Trudi, and who had felt brotherly love for a stranger among them.

Trudi's uncle, an old man, talked briefly of Pa. 'Our brother who came with love among us. Like us, he was a simple man who loved our country.'

I wanted to ask him, 'What could you ever know about my pa?' But instead I joined in the crying, while Pa slipped away to burn.

Everybody cried for Pa, like he was theirs. Trudi looked blonder in deep mourning. I felt alone — really alone. I needed to hear the voice of even one of the women of the yards singing for Pa. I tried to sing but my throat was as dry as a biscuit.

Pa had slipped away to eternity and I knew no more. Jacko later said I had fainted and had to be taken back to the hotel, where I was put to bed. Jacko went to collect Pa's things from Arnie's place, for each item had been allocated to a friend back home. I got out of bed and helped turn out Pa's pockets. In his coat I found a letter addressed to me. Part of it said, 'Arnie is a good son. He is good because of what Trudi is. Her auntie was a brave woman helping to save people from the Nazis. Trudi made her way from the bombed village near the borders, and she found a man from the Gold Coast, and helped him to safety too. She was around thirteen years old. She is not concerned with black and white, just with people. You all hold together. Jacqueline is a true African Eve. Love her! Look after Mattie and understand that Jacko needs loving too. He always has to prove that he's a man. Nobody's ever tender to him, apart from his wife. I know that his pocket is deep, but that should not be the measure of him.'

I did not say anything about the letter to Arnie when that afternoon Jacko and I dropped in to say goodbye. Bitterness still engulfed me and I could not thank Arnie for looking after his own, old father.

We returned to London next day, and Jacko went on to Guyana taking Pa's ashes with him. I heard that a crowd came to meet Pa's ashes with hymn-singing and joy for his long life, and a minister, whose father had been to school with Pa, had led the service.

CHAPTER 10

My house was decorated with condolence cards and I felt comforted when I read the messages inside them. Boscoe was my supporting arm. We read prayers for Pa's soul for nine nights and held a thanksgiving service at the Church of God.

One night I said, 'Boscoe, do you think I should write Arnie a letter thanking him for looking after my father?'

'Oh,' he said, 'Surely *not*. They should be glad they had a father. I wish I had a father.'

I had kept this knowledge from him for years. Was I right to go on doing that? How many silly secrets had gone with my pa? It was then that I told Boscoe where his father lived.

'It was secret,' I said. 'Social Services should be the ones to tell you.' I never asked him what he would do about the knowledge. I resisted interfering in his decisions at all times.

My health had been shaken by Pa's death. I felt weak and slept badly. I decided then that in a year or so's time I would definitely wind down my vocation. By that time Boscoe would be ready to go to stage school and then, if he was lucky, into a repertory company. I could then decide what to do with the rest of my life. In the meantime, I would have the house valued, in case I wanted to sell it and find somewhere smaller.

But in the meantime, a dear little boy called Lloyd was brought to me. He was three years old — a dot in the span of human life span. He was a wiry, brown-eyed, chocolate-skinned child, clinging and complaining in turn. His mother was very sick and could not look after him, for excruciating pain and drugs had crippled her body and her will. His grandmother had taken his older brother to her heart, but she did not want the baby, because her only daughter's illness coincided with his birth. Lloyd loved his grandmother and clung to her, which made matters worse.

'He's like a leech,' she said. 'I can't have that. I have my life to live.' She did not add, 'in the bingo hall', which was her twice-daily indulgence. I took him to my heart at once. I still needed to love and receive the unconditional love which only the youngest children could give. I tried to talk to him, play games with him and hug him, but he responded by almost biting off my little finger with his small, sharp teeth. I was sure that his early emotional life had been even more barren than mine.

He was admitted to a nursery class and at last began to settle. At first he painted pictures in deepest black. He smeared his face and his hair with black paint and painted formless blobs in black and mauve, understood only by him, but gradually his grief faded and colour began to appear in his paintings. His confusions began to clear and he painted shapes and distinct forms. The nursery teacher told me that in his play he had moved away from the dolls' house, the coveted role of mother, and the need always to be wheeling the baby to the shops.

He suddenly began to talk of his mum being dead. Boscoe showed him a dead bird.

'That is dead. Your mum is not dead. She can walk and will come soon.'

'Naw, she's dead.' But Boscoe was more prophetic than he could have guessed. The mother's cancer went into remission, and she came to fetch Lloyd and take him home. He hugged her tightly, speechless for a long while. Then he smiled broadly and yelled, 'Mum! Mum! You Mum, you!'

Jacko wrote me a long, comforting letter, telling me to

listen quietly for Pa's voice when weeds instead of flowers bloomed in my garden. He said that, immediately on his return, a restaurant had fallen into his lap — for a song! Then came the real point of his letter. 'I want kindly care for my family, Sis. Someone Mary-May and I could trust. Would you come, Sis?'

This request was a real shock to me. In the past Jacko had only kept up the occasional correspondence with me, though we had grown closer over Pa's funeral. I remembered Pa's letter to me, how he had written about no one being tender to Jacko except his wife. Now here he was asking for my help. I needed to think about this carefully, and anyway, I could not give up my work right away.

I wrote back to Jacko telling him that I needed time to think about his request.

The very next week the social worker climbed out of her car trailing a young and very attractive girl. She was dishevelled and badly needed a wash. But anyone could see that she had known better days. She was from a family who had been scattered. The father and son had gone to Africa and the three girls had been left to fend for themselves in a squat. The older sisters blamed their youngest sister, the fourteen-year-old, for the break-up, for it was she who had alerted her father to the mother's affair with her young lodger. The father resented being cuckolded and left. Mother fled, too, with her lover, and the sisters, falling on hard times, borrowed money from a merchant of evil and used their young sister as security. Each day the man collected her from school by car and took her off to work in his fields of damnation.

'What made you do it?' I asked.

'We owed him money. I must not shame my father's name by refusing.'

'Tell the police then!'

'I can't shame my father's name. The paper will come and take photographs and there will be my family's face.'

'Say no to evil. You must be strong.'

'I can't. He beats me. He handcuffs me. He will burn me! Kill me!'

'Then where will be your father's name?'

'I will be dead. I will not bear the blame of my father's name being spoiled.'

She went on to tell me that she did not tell the social-work woman because she was white, 'and white people put black people in jail, take away children and laugh at the poor'.

I was in a quandary. I either had to betray her confidence or send her back to her fate. I thought of my own childhood hungers and injustices, and remembered myself, downtrodden, monochrome in my feelings — and desperate in my hopelessness.

What was I to do? This was not an "of course" situation — the women of the yards would avow that. I decided I must disclose the whole situation to the social services director, begging discretion and demanding confidentiality. The girl was in need of safety and care and they were responsible for her, a minor. She was sent to a boarding school.

The man was subsequently arrested. The case could not be proved against him but he was found to be an over-stayer and deported. Ipule continued her schooling and later admitted that the man had, all along, been a relative. It was the final blow to make me lose faith in humanity and I suddenly became sick, collapsed and was admitted to hospital.

Boscoe, sensible and efficient, sent for Lizza once more. She had indeed found a good husband who allowed her to come to our rescue again, bringing in tow her by now overweight and chatty son, Zimri.

I had cared for many, but at that time I felt the need to be cared for. I had never been truly loved nor nurtured in my life, except by Mrs Penn. Relaxing, doing nothing and not using my hands to swing from one tree to another — all were difficult for me, but I read, and I wrote about times good and bad, living through feelings of both anger and laughter. In the process I started to become a person to myself, still pained, but sometimes worthy and good, sometimes not. I tried to sum up my feelings in a poem I wrote on a day when I felt lost, unforgiven and a refugee from family love.

Fate,
You sent this child, a girl,
into the world.
She grew intelligent and capable
With creative resilience.
You cast her untutored
into the ongoing stream of life.
It bore her through the waters of
Infancy and childhood,
Careers, foster-motherhood.
Waged work, and then
To this fraught time.

There is sadness here and gentle pleasures
With anxiety and strife between.
Lonely souls laugh their tears,
Sing creaking melodies and
Pale duets for one,
Share bleary memories
of remembered times.
While mouthing litanies as they await
Those who never come.

In that hoary estuary
Where tired waves bob and break
Over remnants from a former time,
And where on sunny days pebbles
clatter as they move,
And the winds play strange harmonies,

She waits for what is to come,
Wondering when Fate
Will place her soul like a letter
upon another route.

One evening Boscoe appeared at my bedside, beside him a tall, upstanding man whom I did not at first recognise.

'Auntie,' Boscoe said. 'Here is my dad. He has a wife and I have two brothers. My dad wants to thank you for caring for me.'

He had found his family and my heart leapt for the joy of it. Later, Boscoe played Dilly's record to his new family. I had shed so many tears in childhood that they did not come easily to me now. I simply winked at them in my happiness.

I was discharged from hospital after nearly three weeks. My blood pressure had adjusted and I looked forward even more to winding down my fostering. Arnie had heard of my illness and was coming to visit. There was another letter, without a stamp but with a crown on it. I viewed it with deep suspicion. I had fostered around fifty children. I had not killed any of them.

I opened the letter slowly, trying consciously to breathe, to control my blood pressure.

I gave a little cry. The Queen, wonder of wonders, had heard of my work and my love of children. Who had told her? I could not tell! I was insignificant and was happy to be so, but the Queen was going to present me with the Member of the British Empire. I never in my wildest dreams thought she would trouble about me. Blacks always got crumbs or nothing. I called out to Boscoe and he rushed downstairs to congratulate me.

'Auntie,' he said, 'you deserve it. You deserve it more than anyone else. I never heard you condemn a child or destroy their sense of wonder — you took away only their pain. You keep feelings intact and changed the bad ones for better.'

Olive and many of the older children I had fostered came to congratulate me. I took down the condolence cards and displayed my congratulations. Mr Downer, now married to his wife's sister, came with his stylish, grown-up daughters to thank me and wish me well. All I had done was to do the best I could, and behave as Mrs Penn, Mama Tat and the other women of the yards had taught me. I had learned never to treat children as Ma had treated me. I was of her family but not of her womb. Pa had led me to patience and gentleness, but I felt my honour especially for Mrs Penn. She had knowledge but never the opportunity to travel far. She used her gifts to raise people up, to give inspiration and to help men and women do work she could never have dreamed of. I wrote a long letter to Arnie telling him when to come with Trudi and the children. When they came they all accompanied me to visit the Queen. Jacko and the twins had a party for me in New York, and Mattie had one in the yard. Everybody celebrated with rum, song and dance for me.

As for me, my photograph was in the local papers and the glow lasted for days. Arnie and his family arrived two weeks later. Trudi kissed me warmly. I did not squirm — I did not feel I would be burnt or bitten. There was no rancour now.

'I'm glad we are at peace and both our hearts are quiet,' she said. 'I miss your pa so much. I think of him walking by the river. But he is in Heaven, with my parents.'

I smiled. At last we both acknowledged that heaven was common ground.

I dreamed of Pa one night. He seemed pleased about something. Perhaps it was being with Ma and Trudi's parents. Heaven is indeed for those who talk of love and children. Mama Tat and poor neglected Mrs Walker and Mrs Penn are also there, laughing and chatting, eating mangoes and drinking coconut water with the angels.

But there was still the business of Jacko and his invitation. Change had always been difficult for me. Yet sooner or later I would have to decide — and there was still a lot of detritus in my body and mind about my family who had once used me so harshly. I trotted through the days, turning over resolutions and possibilities — waiting for the decision to come. The women of the yards were always with me in thought, but in their silence I began to think they must have fallen asleep.

SECTION 6

Sudden as a storm it came,
News from
Sources known to me.
It touched my every nerve,
Led me into
Grief's drab labyrinth,
Void's sightless pain,
Unexpectedly, like rain,
Leaden, with rainbow frill
Around its moon.
Inchoate,
Uncertain: like me.

CHAPTER 11

Everyone now showed me good will, allowing me a choice of rose-coloured spectacles to view my world. But this made me as unsteady as August corn and, every so often, the bewildered child I had been popped up. At times, I felt I had been cast in the granite of maltreatment, leaving me only obligations and compliance. Yet, at other times I knew I had grown durable, versatile wings that had borne me beyond past occasions, across chasms and seas, precipices and fields, away from the home which like a hound stalked my every step. But my heart still cried out to be as well regarded by my sisters and brothers as I was by others. That was the downside of my award upon me. Thoughts of my painful childhood began to dog my every step, and I imagined old familiar places, and things I had done or had failed to do.

I recalled staring at my image in the stream — into my own brown eyes, a bucket a fantastic crown upon my head. Then Arnie would creep up beside me and shatter the unkempt beauty of that gypsy, simply by dropping a pebble or two into her face. The very centre of her reality would disintegrate until the turbulence died away and there she stood surprised, her senses weak as water. Such thoughts had even sapped my happiness on that day when, dressed in my homely best, I had received my honour.

Memory after memory emerged and then melted away like morning dew. Pushing pain aside, I thought once again of my luck, and counted my blessings. My ears are extremely sharp but I did not hear a single sound when a letter dropped on the floor. It was as if, like a cockroach, it had crept in through the crack under the door.

I finished my coffee and then opened the letter bearing the New York postmark, idly wondering whose handwriting it could be. The shock I got was so big and strong it shook me, blood and bones.

'Oh God!' I cried. 'Jacko! Jacko has been shot!'

The shock of it was like drawing a tooth without anaesthetic. Jacko was to me invulnerable, indestructible, always dressed in God's invisible armour. How could he be shot? It had to be family — one of those gigolo husbands of the twins, I was certain. My anger made me speculate wildly. I had come face to face and heart to heart with a 'not of course' situation. I became a woman of the yards at that moment — my emotions in control of my thoughts. The faces of the twins' husbands kept passing before me. Every time I thought, 'Guilty. Guilty. Guilty. Guilty!'

I sat down, my whole body rigid. Harming Jacko was destroying all that should have been sprinkled, little by little, on all five of us.

I knocked on Boscoe's door. 'I have to go to America,' I said quietly. 'Jacko has been shot.'

There were no tears. I could feel them struggling to the surface, and then receding into those crevices of pain from which they had originally come. My answer to every question was, 'I don't know' and in all honesty I did not know, nor could I imagine how such a disaster could have overtaken poor Jacko.

I found myself searching for something I could not name — pulling drawers open, banging them shut, looking under papers, under cards, leaflets, cuttings. Then I realised I was trying to find a photograph of Jacko, whole and handsome and without injury. But it was Arnie that I found each time. Arnie was everywhere. I did not have a single photograph of Jacko. Yet I had always remembered him, loved him, prayed for him.

I rushed out to the travel agents in my high street but they had closed and it took me another day to get a flight. At least now, though, I was not as worried about leaving my home as I had previously been. Boscoe and Olive could cope with anything.

It was my first confrontation with the mystery of the gun. I could not imagine how a cautious man like Jacko had come to be 'shot'. But of course, I had never been to New York. I began to panic. No one knew I was on my way. But then, dangerous or not, Pa had coped there. So would I, but how did being shot feel? What conversations did the bullet hold with blood and bone? Was it worse than the cutlass cruelties of the yard?

When I arrived, I made rapid progress through customs and then, joy of joy, the twins had come to meet me. Boscoe had had the foresight to cable them the time of my arrival. I still, however, felt confused and depressed, worrying about Jacko, but the twins did not seem to be overconcerned about the event. In answer to my questions, they explained that some 'asshole' had come into the restaurant, demanding money, and when Jacko said, 'Hell, no! You —,' the man, cool as you like, shot him, shattering a shoulder blade and nicking his lungs. Someone had called the police and they surrounded the place. The man had come out fighting and the officers . . . 'blew him away'. I felt a slight guilt at having judged one of the twins' husbands as killer, but I put a brave face on it.

I didn't like the twins facility with rude words and their blasé attitude to other people's misery. I glanced at them between my own higgledy-piggledy thoughts and feelings. Here they were, two middle-aged women, still acting like teenagers. They looked chic. They looked smart, always looking for the main chance. They were strange, like two feather dusters that never touched dust.

I sat there tense, unable to smile at the stories of chicanery, dishonesty and plunder that the twins said were constantly happening in New York. I suppose such things occurred in London too, but they must have passed me by. They say, 'What goes by you is not for you'. The twins continued to entertain and engage each other with stories until we arrived at Jacko's house.

Jacko lived a beautiful part of Brooklyn, for so it could be described in those days. Mary-May, exhausted from lack of sleep, lay on a sofa allowing her three-year-old to nurture her and her eleven-month-old to crawl all over her.

'I'm glad to see you, sister Melda. Jacko would be glad to see you too,' she said. 'He can't talk much as yet, and still sweats with pain. Come with me later on to see him. He had six pints of blood from all of us. He had family blood.'

I sat by her and, to break the gathering silence, said, 'You must really like this house.'

'I don't know, really. But Jacko does.'

'And you?' I thought inwardly. 'What about you? Think for yourself!'

Jacko's house was spacious, with bedrooms, drawing room and family room and all other conveniences upstairs, and a cosy apartment and garage downstairs. I never saw such a place in my life and wondered how they had got used to it.

Mary-May got up and changed her clothes — doing herself up as if for a party.

'Don't forget Jacko is sick,' I warned her. 'He won't be able to dance with you.' She grinned, showing her beautiful teeth against her smooth, dark face.

When we arrived at the hospital, visitors had come by the dozen to stand outside and pray with us. Mishaps, weddings, funerals and dances were good times to see home-people, to gratify nostalgia, as well as friendship. And of course, there was politics to talk about, especially the way things were turning bad back home after independence. It didn't matter to me, and I suppose not to Jacko either, for he loved being in America, making deals and taking chances. I was sure, even as he lay there, that business matters occupied his mind. He smiled at Mary-May and gave the thumbs-up sign. Then he winked at me in the old Jacko manner and gestured about being fed-up and bored.

He could not speak except in a whisper, but squeezed my hand to let me know how pleased he was to see me. 'Make yourself comfortable in my house,' he mouthed. 'I love it.'

'Mary-May look nice,' I replied. 'She dressed for a party. Look at her!'

Jacko smiled and closed his eyes slowly and deliberately as if reluctant to give up the sight of us. I felt a lump in my throat. My poor wounded brother!

Jacko mouthed, 'Have you asked her yet?'

Mary-May turned to me and said, 'Will you come to stay with us? We bought this house when we decided to ask you to come and live with us. Ma asked Jacko to make it up to you. He promised Ma. Will you come?'

'You have your own mother, Mary-May. What about her? She would want her grandchildren. You should have her here.'

'Mama is too old. She wants to go home. This country is purgatory to her. Every New Year's Day she wears mourning.'

'What made her come to America?'

'Same as your pa. To pick up the scraps from the rich man's table. They never told us that table-scraps were gone and only the trash-cans were left for the poor. We worked hard. We scrimped and saved. We ate crow.'

'You have a fine home, Mary-May. I wonder what our ma would say and the women of the yards — Red Daisie, Mama Tat and Auntie Bet? What would all those people, who had picked Arnie as the family winner, say now? Jacko has found the American dream.'

She smiled a thousand words. 'I was afraid to come here,

but Jacko had strength for both of us, though when we were first married he use to wake up crying like a child,' Mary-May whispered.

'Jacko crying?'

'Yes. But he never told me why he cried. Maybe he was afraid to fail.'

Like Pa said, "Money should not be the measure of Jacko". He too needed love. He hid his desires, his needs and his fears from all of us. After all, he was man of the yards. And then there was the example of Pa, who despised dependency upon women and would have died rather than let Ma work for him. He was the man. The earner, the provider. That was what fatherhood meant.

CHAPTER 12

Jacko's request for me to leave London placed me in a dilemma. I was known in my street, to social services, to the people in my church, the doctor, the paper-boy, the butcher and the Greek from whom I bought my black-eyed peas.

Going to America was to become an immigrant all over again, to go through the process of re-establishing myself, of becoming another species, to compromise and recycle or reprocess myself. I was nearly over the hill, in danger of becoming an old maid. Yet, on the other hand, with Jacko there would be ease, whilst in London, my work exhausted me — a patchwork quilt of children's feelings — sometimes love, sometimes resentment, but mostly tolerance, when to them I was the best of a bad lot of choices. There was an earthquake inside me. I decided to wait until it subsided, though there was a brackish feeling in my mouth from the pressure on me.

I called it the feeling of the yards when women waited for voices from inside them to talk to them about what they should do. Then Boscoe wrote to say that the estate agent who'd valued my house had an interested buyer, and that Olive had applied for and obtained a post in a hospital in Newark. God was at work in my life.

Once more I visited Jacko in hospital. He had improved enormously and was being fed fluids. I had promised to read to him. I asked for suggestions from the twins but it was like pulling nails out of dry wood with your fingers. So I asked Mary-May, who said he loved children's stories and Aesop's fables because they reminded him of Pa's talk. What struck me was that no member of the family really knew Jacko. No one had ever paid the real *him* any mind. Jacko gave and we took.

'Well, Aesop was a slave. They say he was an Ethiopian. His name means that. Mrs Penn told me,' I said. 'I'll read him fables of patience and cunning. He would like those. But we stretch out our hands to take from him; we should try to find out something more about him and his needs.'

He was always there for us — solid, dependable and reliable. Like a safe rock in a raging sea. All of us thought of Ma for prayer, Pa for patience, and Jacko for pence when need struck.

I watched Jacko getting slowly better and was delighted the day the X-ray showed his lungs had healed. The operation on his shoulder was also a success and not long afterwards he was discharged from hospital.

We insisted that he had a long convalescence and, after protesting as much as he could, without effect, he and Mary-May went home to Guyana. He wanted to be with Mattie and the spirits of Ma and Pa. I looked after the girls, with the twins visiting and helping each day.

I was pleasantly surprised to find that once you got past their brash exteriors, life had indeed changed them. They included me in everything and we talked freely of the past. No longer were we antagonists. They seemed to have grown tired of being 'nearly stars, nearly famous', and now found contentment in marriage and socialising. They had made good money for themselves as dancers, and their husbands had good incomes. No more pinching and scraping for them!

We spent many pleasant days talking, reliving moments and turning over memories — some of which bit like soldier ants or stung like wasps. I talked of Ma's callous treatment and also of their disregard of me, the name calling, the accusations and the injustices. I talked of the goats again, and they said, with strange logic, 'It couldn't happen in America', which, of course, did not explain why it happened at all.

'We were jealous of you,' they finally confessed. 'Ma took notice of you even if she beat you. You know Ma never hugged us, comforted us — loved us. That's why we clung together, going from guy to guy, in despair. We amused ourselves and we gave amusement. We were hungry for care and love.'

'Ma did what she knew, and taught us what she had learned. I was the one she loathed. She couldn't help herself. Maybe I looked too much like Pa or my mother. Being unkind to me was her way of getting back at him for being unfaithful,' I said.

'We got the nagging — "Milk the goats", "Bathe you skin", "Wipe you neck-back!",' Florizel said.

'We remember Ma. You can remember Ma and Mrs Penn,' added Flora. 'I used to ask God to make Ma lie down and never more get up. And Florizel used to beat me for saying that.'

'When we visited you in London and I saw your house, I felt thrilled for you, Melda, but was I jealous!' said Florizel. 'And Mama Tat used to call for *you* to go with her to the women's needle party. I would have given anything to go.'

I told them of the day I first went with Mama Tat to a shack where the women were making what they called a 'rose bedspread'. They had brought circles of bright material which they gathered together into "roses" with a tiny hole in the centre. These they sorted and ironed carefully. I watched the gentle work, the complex business of designing the bedspread, the tacking, and sewing the "roses" together. 'We make this for a wedding,' Mama Tat explained. 'It will look nice. You can use it on both sides — one with gathers, the other side flat. It is a thing heavy with love.'

I remembered bursting out, 'I will never have one! Everyone hates me. They all hate me. God never even gave me a mother! I am ugly! Look at me!' Following these bitter words, tears burst the dam inside me. I yelled and rolled about inconsolably. Mama Tat hugged me. 'Don't talk so,' she begged. There was hair in her armpits and I pulled at it out of spite. She pulled away. 'Oooh!' she yelled. 'Gal, you so bad.

Gawd pretect me liver from you!' I ran all the way home.

The twins and I laughed ourselves to tears, and we shared more stories of Mama Tat. Then I said, 'Jacko wants me to come to live here.'

For a change they looked serious, exchanged glances and said, 'Mary-May is a nice girl — she wants help and we worry that you live over there with no family. We want you to come and be with us, like a true sister.'

'You mean that? Even though Ma was not my real mother. You count me as a sister?'

'Of course, we count you. And you look like Pa. What happened long ago is nothing to do with us. Judge not lest ye be judged.'

'Jacko is coming home in two days' time, and I will agree to come and live with them, and help the children. I will say yes.'

My twin sisters both gave an uninhibited shout of joy and, although only God and the two children were present, they had, by doing so, openly owned me. I was somebody now. I belonged, and for all of us and indeed for our ancestors that is a significant part of our identity.

At once we began preparing for a wonderful reunion, with food and music and dancing. We would call upon the spirits of the women of the yards to attend and our ma and pa would be there. Pa smiling and Ma — well, no one could tell.

Little Emelda and baby Lisette started clapping their hands, joining in the warmth of the feeling and affection without knowing why. Like Arnie's and Trudi's children they will inherit another time — hopefully without want or cruelty or anguish. They should never know the pain that can strangle the desire to love and to give.

For me, perhaps, the search was coming to an end, and my whole scrambled world was swinging into clearer focus. The clouds were breaking up. My wounds were healing. I saw a beautiful and happy girl smiling up at the sun from the bottom of the rainwater barrel.

Green Grass Tango

Alfred Grayson, a retired and widowed civil servant, decides to buy a dog to try 'not to be so lonely'. Sheba is his passport to the richly multi-racial community of dog-walkers and bench-sitters who meet in a down-at-heel London park. Here Grayson engages with cunning Finbar, theatrical Arabella and her absurd tango-dancing sidekick Harold Heyhoe, Jamaican Maryanne tortured by her demons, Rastafarian Rootsman, old Uncle Nat from Sierra Leone, tattoed Judy and abandoned Lucy.

Grayson, originally from Barbados, has passed for white and kept his origins quiet during his civil service career. But when he tries to befriend Maryanne and she remains suspicious, thinking him English and white, he begins to rethink his past.

In the park, characters, who would not otherwise meet, make unlikely alliances and feel able to expose various identities, or in Alfred's case begin to reconstruct one. Both park and characters have their times of shabbiness and moments of blooming glory.

This is comedy filled with a sense of human fragility and impermanence.

Price: £7.95
ISBN: 1 900715 47 3

Sunlight on Sweet Water

Beryl Gilroy transports the reader back to the Guyanese village of her childhood to meet such characters as Mr Dewsbury the Dog Doctor, Mama Darlin' the village midwife and Mr Cumberbatch the Chief Mourner.

It was a time when 'children did not have open access to the world of adults and childhood had not yet disappeared'. Perhaps for this reason, the men and women who pass through these stories have a mystery and singularity which are as unforgettable for the reader as they were for the child. Beryl Gilroy brings back to life a whole, rich Afro-Guyanese community, where there were old people who had been the children of slaves and where Africa was not forgotten.
Sunlight on Sweet Water is fast becoming a Peepal Tree best-seller and is widely taught on women's and Caribbean literature courses.

Price: £6.95
ISBN: 0 948833 64 5

Inkle and Yarico

being the narrative of Thomas Inkle concerning his shipwreck and long sojourn among the Caribs and his marriage to Yarico, a Carib woman.

As a young man of twenty, Thomas Inkle sets out for Barbados to inspect the family sugar estates. On the way he is shipwrecked on a small West Indian island inhabited by Carib Indians. He alone escapes as his shipmates are slaughtered, and is rescued by Yarico, a Carib woman who takes him as, "an ideal, strange and obliging lover." So begins an erotic encounter which has a profound effect on both. Amongst the Caribs, Inkle is a mere child, whose survival depends entirely on Yarico's protection. But when he is rescued and taken with Yarico to the slave island of Barbados, she is entirely at his mercy.

Inkle and Yarico is loosely based on a "true" story which became a much repeated popular narrative in the 17th and 18th centuries. Beryl Gilroy reinterprets its mythic dimensions from both a woman's and a black perspective, but above all she engages the reader in the psychological truths of her characters' experiences.

As an old man, Inkle recalls the Carib's stories as being like 'fresh dreams, newly washed, newly woven and true to the daily lives of the community'. Inkle and Yarico has the same magic and pertinence.

This is a narrative of deep historical insight into the commodifying and abuse of humanity and an excellent book for close study in schools and colleges. Gilroy lays the past bare as a text for the present.

Price: £6.95
ISBN: 0 948833 98 X

Gather the Faces

Marvella Payne is twenty-seven, works as a secretary for British Rail and has pledged to the congregation of the Church of the Holy Spirit that she will abstain from sex before marriage. When she repulses the groping hands of the trainee-deacon, Carlton Springle, she resigns herself to growing old with her mother, father and Bible-soaked aunts. But Aunt Julie has other ideas and finds Marvella a penfriend from her native Guyana. When good fortune allows the couple to meet, Marvella awakens to new possibilities as she realises how bound she has been by the voices of her dependent, cossetted childhood. But will marriage be another entrapment, another loss of self?

Price£6.99
ISBN 0-948833-88-2

About Peepal Tree Press

In the nineteenth century over two million Indians were lured away to work as indentured labourers on the sugar estates of the Caribbean, Mauritius, Fiji and other parts of the Empire. They brought the peepal tree with them and planted in these new environments, a sign of their commitment to their cultural roots.

Peepal Tree focuses on the Caribbean and its Diaspora, and also publishes writing from the South Asian Diaspora and Africa. Its books seek to express the popular resources of transplanted and transforming cultures.

Based in Leeds, Peepal Tree began humbly in a back bedroom in 1986, and has now published over 100 quality literary paperback titles, with fiction, poetry and literary, cultural and historical studies. We publish around 15 English language titles a year, with writers from Guyana, Jamaica, Trinidad, Nigeria, Bangladesh, Montserrat, St Lucia, America, Canada, the UK, Goa, India and Barbados.

Peepal Tree is committed to publishing writing which explores new areas of reality which is multi-ethnic and multicultural. We aim to publish writing of high literary merit which 'makes a difference', which challenges assumptions and leads to cross-cultural understanding. Our list contains work by established authors such as Kamau Brathwaite, Beryl Gilroy, Ismith Khan and David Dabydeen (and lots more!), but we are also strongly committed to publishing new writers.

Feel free to contact us for information about our books and writers and we'll do our best to help. We also offer a full mail order service to anywhere in the world.

Peepal Tree Press, 17, Kings Avenue, Leeds LS6 1QS, United Kingdom
tel +44 (0113) 2451703 e-mail <hannah@peepal.demon.co.uk>
website (from May 2002) http://www.peepaltreepress.com